CORINTHIAN'S KISS

"And why should a bluestocking care what a Corinthian thinks? I would guess that a word of concern from my lips would hardly be enough to dissuade you from your intellectual pursuits."

His words only made her aware of how close his lips were to her own. "Quite . . . quite right," she stammered. This was not at all what she had had in mind. She was losing control of the situation. And he was entirely too close. However, her attempts to move away only brought her up against the refreshment cart. She stumbled, and he caught her in his arms.

Jenny gazed up at him. She could feel the strength of him around her, the warmth of his embrace. He was smiling down at her almost tenderly, and she realized he was actually going to kiss her moments before his lips brushed hers.

She had never been kissed before, not by her suitors during her come-out year, certainly not by those who had sought her out since. Nothing prepared her for Kevin's kiss. It was sweet, it was warm, it was infinitely pleasurable. More, it filled her with a longing to stay this way forever. When he raised his head to gaze down at her, it was all she could do not to pull him to her again.

"I think, Miss Welch," he said softly with a gentle smile, "that we have found one area in which we suit admirably . . ."

Books by Regina Scott

THE UNFLAPPABLE MISS FAIRCHILD
THE TWELVE DAYS OF CHRISTMAS
THE BLUESTOCKING ON HIS KNEE

Published by Zebra Books

THE BLUESTOCKING ON HIS KNEE

Regina Scott

Zebra Books
Kensington Publishing Corp.
http://www.zebrabooks.com

ZEBRA BOOKS are published by

Kensington Publishing Corp.
850 Third Avenue
New York, NY 10022

Copyright © 1999 by Regina Lundgren

Zebra and the Z logo Reg. U.S. Pat. & TM Off.

First Printing: May, 1999
10 9 8 7 6 5 4 3 2 1

Printed in the United States of America

To my father Richard P. Brown and my husband Larry, who know the value of intelligent women; and to Kate McMurry, an incorrigible bluestocking in her own right, for sharing her boxing research.

One

After hours of poring over the figures of his much-diminished finances, Kevin Whattling pushed back one of the last three of his mahogany dining chairs, rose, and stretched. Giles Sloane and Sir Nigel Dillingham, his very best friends in the world, stared up at him, dazed. Nigel shook his close-cropped, sandy blond head.

"Don't see how you can be so relaxed, old man," he frowned. Since Nigel's eyebrows were remarkably bushy and his nose singularly imposing, his frowns were known to curdle milk. Kevin merely shrugged.

"I agree, Kevin," Giles chimed in. "I've known you to face calamity with a laugh, but this . . . this is something else entirely." His round face under a thatch of red hair and equally round frame were more likely to be found consuming milk than curdling it. Nonetheless, his chubby cheeks, pale and quivering, had more effect on his friend than Nigel's heavy frowns.

Kevin clapped him on the shoulder. "Buck up, my lad. Things may look a trifle difficult . . ."

"A trifle!" Nigel rumbled. "Penury he calls a trifle!"

Giles snatched the cross-hatched piece of paper off the table and bent over it again, pudgy fingers running down the columns. "Perhaps we subtracted incorrectly. Is that it, Kev? Tell me you have other assets. Perhaps a rich uncle you never told us about?"

Kevin smiled ruefully. "Sorry, Giles. Everything I have is written on that sheet. And as you can see, I am completely penniless. The very furniture on which you sit will be auctioned off tomorrow. And that doesn't count the two thousand still owed to George Safton, not that I begrudge making him sing for it."

"Gads!" Nigel gasped.

Giles shuddered. "If only we could help you out. But my inheritance barely covers expenses."

Nigel eyed his friend's considerable bulk. "We all know where your funds go, old fellow. As I don't eat mine, I have a bit more to spare. I can spot you enough to keep up the rent on your rooms for a month or so, Kevin. Unfortunately, I don't have enough to pay off Safton, worse luck."

Kevin shrugged again. "You needn't bother, Nigel." Now that he knew the worst of it, he found it difficult to be morose. There was a strange sort of freedom, not having to keep up appearances any longer. He reached to the center of the small table and poured three goblets of port from the decanter there. Passing them to his friends, he raised his own in a toast.

"Gentlemen, have no fear! As Napoleon was defeated so recently on the Peninsula, so shall we defeat this specter of poverty. To success!"

"Here, here!" Giles chimed in. He dashed back the port, obviously carried away by Kevin's show of enthusiasm.

Nigel humphed and sipped his instead. "You're mighty cheerful for a man so deep in Dun Territory."

"That, my dear Nigel, is because I have a plan."

Giles poured himself another glass with glee. "I knew it! Trust Kevin to think his way out of any scrape."

Nigel eyed his friend dubiously, gray eyes shrewd. "A plan, have you? You aren't exactly known for planning. Besides, what, pray tell, could you possibly plan that could raise the necessary blunt? I thought you'd sworn off gambling. Or did you give in to Safton's lures?"

Kevin raised an expressive eyebrow. "Do you think so little of me as that, Nigel?"

Nigel had the good sense to study his port while answering. "It isn't a matter of what I think. Giles and I both told you what a loose fish George Safton was, manipulative, conniving wretch. There's a good reason the ton calls him The Snake. But you weren't ready to pay us much heed until . . ." He shifted in his seat, twirling the cut-glass stem of the goblet between long fingers. "Sorry. Unsportsmanlike of me. Never mind."

"You don't have to be afraid to say it," Kevin replied, fingering the black armband and making sure neither of his friends saw what an effort his nonchalance cost him. "If I had listened to either of you, Robbie might still be alive."

"Oh, Kevin, never say so!" Giles defended him, blue eyes wide. "You did what you could. You know I thought quite highly of your brother, but he simply couldn't turn down a wager. And Safton can't turn down an easy mark. They were the worst possible combination. But you mustn't see it as your fault that your brother was led astray."

"Only that I did part of the leading," Kevin reminded him. "I introduced him to Safton. I never thought to pass along your warnings. I paid his debts again and again with no more than a brotherly scold. I even went along with most of their ridiculous schemes."

"So did half of the ton," Nigel put in. "You have to give them this—they were an entertaining pair."

"Until the very end," Giles agreed, but he shuddered again.

"You don't have to wrap it up in clean linen, gentlemen," Kevin insisted. "I have nothing to say in my own defense. I've been an idiot and a dastard. I've lost my only brother, nearly ruined our family name, and run myself nicely into Dun Territory. In short, I've made a mess of my life and now I have the ignominious pleasure of trying to get myself out of it."

"Which you'll do with style and wit," Giles assured him.

Kevin spread his hands. "Is there any other way?"

"This is getting us nowhere," Nigel grumbled. "You said you had a plan. Will you tell us about it, or not?"

Giles suddenly looked worried. "You didn't apply to those advertisements in *The Times,* did you, Kevin? I shouldn't think a gentleman could find suitable work that way."

"You'd be surprised what one can find in *The Times,*" Kevin told him ruefully. "Unfortunately, all the responses I received indicated that there was nothing a failed Corinthian was suitable for. You would hardly hire me for a companion, and I'm far past the appropriate age for an apprentice for any trade. Of course, I can always work below stairs. I'd make a strapping footman, don't you think?"

This time both Nigel and Giles shuddered.

"Do not fear, gentlemen," Kevin told them in consolation. "I have decided on a less onerous approach." He felt sure enough of himself to grin at both his friends, pausing dramatically until he was certain he had their full attention.

"Gentlemen, I plan to sell the last asset I own—myself. I will marry an heiress."

Giles choked on his port. Nigel gaped, but was the first to recover.

"Nonsense," he snorted.

"Oh, I say, a poor joke, Kev," Giles seconded, mopping wine from the broad front of his linen shirt with a damask handkerchief. He stopped his ablutions long enough to peer up at his friend. "Are you foxed?"

Kevin's grin widened. "Not in the slightest. I know exactly what I am about."

"Can't be done," Nigel proclaimed. "Too much against you."

"Such as?" Kevin challenged.

Nigel ticked his reasons off on his long fingers. "One— you've no title, which the papas of most heiresses hang out for. Two—you've no fortune or estates, although I admit you had a respected family name, if they do not count this recent business. Three—it's well known you've been living beyond your blunt, not to mention your fondness for gaming, boxing, racing, and the muslin company. Four—"

"That's quite enough," Kevin laughed, holding up his hands in surrender. "Your logic is flawless. I have only two small credits to counter your long list of debits. I understand I am considered by the ladies to be reasonably kind on the eyes, and I have been told I possess a certain amount of charm."

Nigel snorted again. Giles cocked his head thoughtfully. Kevin held his smile as they both looked at him with appraising eyes.

He knew the image he presented. At six feet, two inches tall, he towered over both of them, as well as most of the other men in his class. Unlike the thoroughly round Giles or the endlessly angular Nigel, his shoulders were broad enough, his waist narrow enough, and his legs powerful enough to carry off the latest fashion of cutaway coats and skintight breeches with polished style. His practices at Jackson's, although less frequent of late, guaranteed his muscular build. He had heard the rumor that his shock of honey gold hair, which curled in natural artistic disarray, had once caused Lord Byron to sack his valet when that poor worthy failed to match it. His eyes were a deep, warm shade of blue that seemed to invite the ladies to look closer and offer confidences. He thought his high cheekbones, long nose, and slightly pointed chin lent his face character when he was solemn, and they certainly seemed to encourage others to grin along with him when he was pleased about something. One of his favorite opera dancers had told him he could have played Oberon if he had been darker. The thought of playing King of the Fairy World amused him; surely there were worse entities to whom one might be compared. Besides, good looks aside, he had a ready wit and an easy grace. Until the recent incident with his brother, most of his friends would have called him easygoing by nature, which had made him the first person on many a hostess's guest list. Of course, it was that easygoing nature that had landed him in the fix he was in, but he steadfastly pushed that thought aside.

"He has you there," Giles was nodding to Nigel. "Devilishly attractive, that's our Kevin. Seen many a gel swoon at his feet."

Kevin flicked a speck of lint off the lapel of his black evening coat, trying not to show his relief that his friends' assessments matched his own. "Well, perhaps not swoon," he demurred with just the right amount of humility.

"I still say it takes more than good looks and a ready wit to sway an heiress," Nigel insisted doggedly.

Giles had clearly already been won over. "Have you picked the gel yet, Kevin?"

Kevin wandered to the mirror near the door of his small suite of rooms and made himself busy retying his cravat.

He hadn't expected them to be won over quite this quickly. Perhaps his plan wasn't as lack-witted as he had first thought. The true test, however, would be their assessment of the woman he had chosen to pursue. He knew he'd have to face them sooner or later, and decided the time might as well be now. "Yes, though I doubt either of you will approve of my choice."

"Fanny Brighton is tolerable," Giles offered.

"If you don't mind buck teeth and a laugh like a horse's," Nigel complained. "Besides, she wouldn't have you. I have it on good authority that no less than a duke may be offering for her quite soon."

"Evalina Turnpeth, then," Giles suggested.

"Rusticating in the country until the summer," Nigel replied.

"What about that cit Sir John nearly wed?"

"A cit!" Nigel exploded. He threw back the last of his port. "Egad, man, are you mad?"

Giles sank lower in his chair.

Kevin turned to his friends with a rueful smile. "No, not a cit, Nigel, never fear. The lady I have in mind is a blue blood through and through. She also happens to be a bit of a bluestocking as well. I thought I'd try my luck with Eugennia Welch."

"Eugennia Welch!" his friends chorused, their faces awash in horror.

So much for their support. Kevin faced them with determination, refusing to be swayed so easily. "You see, I told you you wouldn't approve."

Again, Nigel recovered first. "I can see the attraction, old fellow. She's known to be quite odd, so you won't have to put up with a lot of nonsense with dresses and balls and the like. But who could stand her insane activities?"

"I don't see them as insane," Kevin protested with a

smile. "What has she done—invited the Egyptian expedition to conduct a practice dig in her rear yard? That seems far more practical than trying to accompany them all the way to Egypt."

"That was nothing compared to the time she descended upon Weston to learn how a man's coat was cut," Nigel declared. "I can still see Lord Bellington's face as he stood there in his short sleeves with Weston pointing out the various tucks needed. Poor Bell hasn't been the same since."

"He was never all that bright to begin with," Kevin shrugged. "Not much of a loss if you ask me."

"And don't forget," Giles put in wide-eyed, "she was the one who convinced the printers to go out on the ice last year when the Thames froze. She claimed the crowds should have something to memorialize their visit to the Frost Fair, as if any of them could read or would know what to do with the paper in the first place."

"I notice you had your leaflet framed, Giles," Kevin pointed out.

"All that aside, Kevin," Nigel insisted, "it is well known she despises everything you stand for—gaming, pugilistic displays, horse racing."

"I'd like to think I stand for a little more than that, Nigel," Kevin chided.

"What else is there?" Nigel demanded.

"Not to mention that she's past her last prayers," Giles chimed in.

"She can't be over six and twenty," Kevin responded. "Lord Davies threw her a quarter-century birthday party—remember how the ladies gasped that anyone would be willing to admit her age in public? It was the same month Robbie arrived in town, and that was nearly a year ago." The thought unnerved him for a moment, as any thought of Robbie was wont to do even three months after his brother's death, but he plunged ahead.

"I've thought this through very carefully, gentlemen. Eugennia Welch has a fortune of forty thousand pounds per annum. She purportedly has withstood offers from an earl and a marquis, so she cannot be hanging out for a title. Her father died six years ago, and she has no other male relatives, so I shall not have to fight a dubious family. She seems to prefer the town life, so my lack of a country seat should not dismay her." He felt his grin reappear as he remembered the last time he had seen her. "Besides, I stood up with her at a country dance last fall, and I rather enjoyed the experience. Despite all your protests, she is a lady through and through. So, unless you have further suggestions, I plan to call on her tomorrow and begin my trip toward the altar."

Giles solemnly poured the last of the port into the three glasses.

"To success?" he offered hesitantly, handing them around.

"No," Kevin corrected, accepting his and raising it high. "To Miss Eugennia Welch. May she soon be the bluestocking on my knee."

"To Miss Welch," Nigel and Giles chorused, and this time all three glasses were enthusiastically drained.

Two

Miss Eugennia Welch made a face at herself in the pier glass mirror on her rosewood dressing table.

"Stop that at once," her companion and abigail, Miss Martha Tindale, sniffed in disapproval. She gave Eugennia's long hair an extra tug with the silver-backed brush she had been pulling through it. "Have you never heard that the good Lord could freeze your face and you'd be stuck that way forever?"

"What a farradiddle," Eugennia scoffed. "I'm quite glad you took up with someone sensible like me. I would hate to hear such nonsense repeated to someone who might actually believe it."

"Humph," came the reply as the older woman busied herself in plaiting the soft light brown tresses for the complex bun Eugennia normally wore. Martha Tindale knew that Jenny Welch was no fool. Indeed, she was in awe of the vast store of knowledge her mistress had amassed from her studies. Martha's head of tight gray curls positively ached just thinking of reading as much as Jenny did. And she would never have had the courage to pursue such studies into the real world. In fact, Martha wasn't entirely sure such studies were proper for a young lady, although she could scarcely tell Eugennia that.

Once the topic had been insects, and Martha had followed Jenny about Hyde Park as her mistress captured a frightening assortment of multilegged creatures to observe. Martha had been sure the horrid things would get loose, and woke repeatedly each night they had been in residence to make sure she hadn't expired from their bites.

Another time it had been heavenly bodies, and Martha had gotten quite tired of being dragged from her bed in the middle of the night to watch for some mysterious event called a comet, which had never appeared. She had much preferred the time Jenny had studied landscape paintings, and they had had the good fortune to tour a number of the local town houses to see some of the fine examples on display there. Accompanying that painter to Kew Gardens to capture a group of trees on canvas had been rather peaceful. If only all of Jenny's studies went so well! Of course, lately, Miss Jenny had been content to stay at home and read quietly, but that only meant that she hadn't found her next passion. Then they would all be off on some new escapade, Martha had no doubt.

She screwed up her long, thin face and narrowed her gray eyes at a recalcitrant strand of hair that seemed determined to evade her. She looked up again in time to see Eugennia pull her tongue quickly back into her mouth. Had she actually been sticking it out at her?

"Well, honestly," Martha sniffed, much annoyed, "why are you so out of countenance today? If you'd like to try another style, you have only to say so."

Jenny looked contrite, plucking at the cream lace on the sleeve of her puce silk morning dress. "I'm sorry, Martha. Don't be vexed with me. This style is fine. It's just that everything is so very predictable—my hairstyle, my days, my life, even your reaction just now. Don't you ever wish things would change?"

"Certainly not!" Martha declared vehemently. "My life

is just right, thank you very much." Seeing the sad expression on Jenny's face, she softened. "But we could try something different with your hair, if you like."

For a moment, Jenny brightened; then the light in her hazel eyes faded and she shrugged. "It doesn't matter, Martha. Changing my hair won't change the way things are." As Martha put the last pin in place, Jenny rose and wandered to the nearby window, parting the blue velvet curtains to gaze down at the small garden behind her town house.

Martha watched her with concern. "But what exactly is wrong, Eugennia? What is it you want to change?"

What indeed, Jenny pondered, watching a stray breeze bend the stalks of the jonquils below her. She ought to be as content as Martha was, even if she hadn't been able to settle her mind on any particular new course of study.

She had certainly attempted to craft a life that would lead to contentment. Although she had dutifully had her come-out and entered the whirl of the Season in her eighteenth year to please a doting father, her father's passing two years later had opened the way for an existence she'd thought would more suit her temperament. In truth, she found very little of interest in the balls and routs and teas she was expected to attend. She felt far more fulfilled conducting intellectual pursuits and sharing her findings with people of similar interests.

In the last six years, she had created a home that contained all the comforts one might need, including a staff who, for the most part, had seen her grow up and were excessively fond of "our Miss Jenny." She had a carefully selected circle of well-read, cultivated friends who visited with just the right frequency so as not to become cloying. She had a wider circle of acquaintances whom she had met through her various studies, including an entomologist, an Egyptologist, and a quartet of musicians who seemed proud to say she sponsored them.

Each room in her home, like the bedroom in which she stood, was decorated in tones of blue and rose and saffron. Each piece of furniture had been handpicked or made to her design. Her bedroom, for example, was done in the Chinese style, with dragons carved on the matching rosewood dressing table, dresser, armoire, and headboard; gold and silver embroidery on the rose satin coverlet, bed hangings, and blue velvet drapes; and gold fans decorating the blue satin-hung walls. The Aubusson carpet beneath her had been commissioned to her specifications to match the room, with a blue and rose dragon at opposite corners, each holding a gold fan.

She had a regimen of activities that included her studies, trips to various booksellers and lending libraries, a daily constitutional, and an occasional cultural event in the evening. Her tremendous fortune left to her by her father ensured that she would want for nothing. Indeed, she had been pleased to use it to purchase a number of unique and notable items that were now scattered about the house in glass cabinets.

But lately the carefully dusted, well-polished glass cases seemed to her to be a symbol of her life. The very things she thought would bring her contentment, instead made her feel trapped, smothered in an airless existence. Even her studies failed to satisfy.

She had never been one for melancholy self-reflection. She found it much easier to analyze a situation or even the reactions of another person than to understand what drove her to act in a particular way. However, she suspected that wanting a different hairstyle this morning was merely a symptom. She had an overwhelming urge to do something radically different, to break the glass that seemed to be hung around her and . . .

And do what? What exactly should she change? She had tried any number of studies, from science to art to history, but none amused her of late. It seemed foolish to throw out her friends or move to the Continent on an emotional whim. Even new clothes seemed a ridiculous waste of her time. She let her eyes focus on the faint reflection of herself in the windowpane. The problem was deeper than a mere change of scene, she felt. Her very image seemed to bother her. But why?

She was no beauty, but neither was she a hag. Her long silken hair framed a face that was distressingly round, not oval, with cheeks that tended to resemble two ripe red apples when she blushed. Her figure and frame were far too rounded to carry off the willowy Grecian look that was all the rage. Her hair was a shade between blond and brunette, and her eyes between blue and brown, as if her coloring was having as difficult a time as her mind in knowing what it wanted. She had large eyes, a stub of a nose, and a generous mouth. In all, she had determined long ago, it was not a picture to inspire a man to poetry.

Good heavens, was that it? She startled involuntarily. Romance and marriage had seemed to pop into her mind with surprising frequency of late. She suspected it was a symptom of her advancing age and the appellation of spinster that seemed to be hanging over her. Yet she had thought she'd put such petty concerns behind her long ago.

Her attempts at the social whirl had been less than successful from the first. She could never bring herself to utter the drivel that young ladies were expected to spout at the least provocation. Any man who could only converse about the weather, his horses, or the latest fashion earned her instant contempt, which she found impossible to conceal. She couldn't paint, her embroidery was a shambles, she was tone deaf, and she had never learned to execute more than a country dance with grace. Yet she forced herself to participate in the meaningless ritual at least twice a year on the conviction that one must contribute to the social order. The carefully chosen ball or rout inevitably left her delighted to return to the simplicity of her everyday existence. Unfortunately, her latest foray into society four months ago had left her unaccountably moody, and she was very much afraid she knew why.

"You told me some nonsense, Martha," she sighed, turning from the window to find her companion looking at her with a worried frown that only made her long nose look longer and her small eyes smaller. "Now I'll tell you some. Do you know what I dream about?"

"No," Martha replied, fascinated. She perched on the edge of the four-poster bed, black bombazine skirts swinging against the rose satin bed cover. "What?"

"A handsome prince. You know, the kind in *The Sleeping Beauty*? We read that story a year or so ago, by Planche."

"French nonsense," Martha sniffed.

Jenny smiled indulgently. "Very well, I read it then, just about the time I also read Perrault's *Fairy Tales*. Both of those books had heroines who are rescued by handsome charming princes, just as I wish to be rescued. Well, perhaps not a prince, precisely. But very handsome. And charming." She tried to think of an image other than the one that had been haunting her, but none other came to mind. "Do you remember the very tall gentleman who asked me to dance at the Baminger ball last November?"

Martha frowned. "Not particularly. Why?"

Jenny returned her frown. "You cannot have missed

him, Martha. He was quite the most presentable man at the ball."

"Well, there were a great many presentable men at that ball, if you ask me," Martha maintained. "You cannot expect me to remember this one over that."

Jenny sighed. "Perhaps he asked me to dance while you were talking to Lord Davies. Miss St. John will surely remember him. To my mind, he was unforgettable."

"What has this to do with the way you feel?" Martha demanded.

"I find myself imagining a prince as handsome and charming as my dance partner," Jenny confided. "Only, in my dreams, he rides up to my doorstep and walks into my sitting room and declares, 'Miss Eugennia Welch, I intend to marry you,' just like that." She giggled, and even to her ears the sound was unexpectedly girlish. Then, seeing Martha's confused expression, she sobered. "Only that is never going to happen. I don't even know the gentleman's name—I was so shocked to be asked to dance that I forgot we weren't introduced. Besides, with this life of mine, I've woven a very effective cocoon about myself, and for all I might turn into a butterfly, I can't get out. Do you understand?"

"No!" Martha slipped off the bed and stalked to the door. "Hairstyles, princes, butterflies. Honestly, Eugennia, sometimes I don't understand a word you say." She turned back to eye her mistress sternly. "All I can say is that you better watch what you wish for—you just might get it!"

Jenny laughed. "Another dire prediction? Oh, Martha, there's precious little fear of my getting my wish. Why, I would more likely be struck by lightning than to have someone suitable propose out of the blue."

Martha clapped her hands over her ears with a shriek.

"Not another word! Think shame on yourself for tempting fate!"

Jenny laughed again and opened her mouth to make another jest, when there was a sudden pounding at her bedroom door. Martha leapt away from it as if it had struck her.

"Who is it?" Jenny called, her heart starting to beat faster.

"Mavis, mum. Mr. Fiching sent me. You have a caller downstairs."

Martha gasped. "See what you've done!"

"Oh, hush," Jenny snapped, patience gone. "It's probably Susan to discuss the next book for the reading circle." She reached for the door handle, and Martha dashed in front of her.

"Don't go, I tell you!" she cried. "It's something dreadful—I can feel it!"

Jenny shook her head, but she raised her voice to speak through the door. "Do you know, Mavis, is it Miss St. John?"

"No, mum," Mavis's voice came back sounding a bit subdued, but it could have been because of the thickness of the door. "Mr. Fiching said it were a gentleman."

Martha braced her thin back against the door, looking like a crow defending a choice morsel. "You see!"

"Oh, Martha, please," Jenny frowned. "Mavis, tell Mr. Fiching I'll be right down." She eyed her distraught companion. "Really, Martha. I promise you it will prove to be someone from a charity, or perhaps a solicitor. Gentleman caller indeed. I'll be through with him in less than a quarter hour, and nothing will have changed. You needn't even bother to come down." She frowned so quellingly that Miss Tindale was forced to move away from the door, though she did so with great trepidation. As she watched her mistress turn the handle, dread seized her anew.

"Jenny, wait!"

Eugennia paused at the door, eyebrow raised.

Martha swallowed. "If it is a handsome prince, wouldn't you like me to change your hair?"

"My hair," Jenny declared, "is just fine, and I defy any prince, handsome or not, to tell me otherwise." And so saying, she sailed out of the room.

Three

Despite her bold declaration, Jenny hesitated in front of the hall mirror and tucked a stray lock in place before moving toward the door to the main salon, where her butler Fiching stood sentry.

"Mr. Kevin Whattling, Miss," he intoned as he reached for the gilt door handle. Then he lowered his voice conspiratorially. "A regular top-o-the-trees Corinthian he is, too, Miss Jenny. Shall I stay, or would you like an excuse to be alone with him for a moment?"

Jenny didn't have the heart to scold him for his lack of protocol; after all, she had known the man since her childhood. What little remained of his hair was white now, and his eyes were buried in wrinkles, although the faded blue still held the twinkle of kindness she remembered. Though his spare frame looked elegant in his black coat and breeches, she knew just how much it cost him to stand so straight when he suffered from rheumatism. "Stay, please, Fiching," she whispered back. "I can't imagine what he could want."

Fiching winked at her.

She composed herself and nodded permission for him to open the door. She could feel him behind her as she came into the room.

Kevin rose to his feet as she entered, and she was hard-pressed not to gasp. It couldn't be! Her legs trembled beneath her, and she had to fight a sudden desire to run back upstairs to Martha. Having only just confessed her obsession with the man, she could not believe that he should suddenly appear in her sitting room.

He was dressed in a cutaway coat of dark blue superfine, with a blue and white striped satin waistcoat peeking out in front. His snowy white cravat, crisp shirt points, and long legs encased in skintight white breeches with shining tasseled Hessians, bespoke the proper gentleman of fashion. She stood there staring, mouth hanging open. A part of her brain warned her she looked significantly less intelligent than she was rumored to be, but she couldn't seem to move to do anything about it.

He bowed. "Miss Welch, how kind of you to receive me."

"Mr. Whattling," Jenny managed, dropping a curtsey and wishing she was wearing something more elegant than her puce silk. "How nice of you to call. To what do I owe this honor?"

He was watching her closely, and now he smiled ruefully. "Ah, you don't remember me, do you?"

Was her confusion so apparent? "Well, perhaps not precisely," she replied, thinking that it was *near* the truth, since she had only just now learned his name.

"Ah, what a leveler," Kevin sighed. "I had so hoped I'd made a lasting impression. We met at the Bamingers' ball last November. You stood up with me for a country dance."

She did not need his reminder to relive the scene. Even then she had been shocked by his regard. All she had managed then was to nod in agreement to his request for a dance. Thankfully, the pattern of the dance had made conversation almost impossible. Yet the few times he had addressed her, she remembered answering in monosyllables. It was little wonder she hadn't remembered to have someone introduce them—she had barely been able to meet his eye. Much as she had wished to meet him again, she could not see how she could have made any kind of impression on him for him to wish to further the acquaintance.

"Yes, of course," she nodded. "It has just been some time, after all."

"But I haven't forgotten you," he replied, surprising her further. "I've thought of you quite often."

"And it's taken you four months to call?" she asked, then felt the blush deepen as she realized how blunt she sounded.

Straight-faced, he replied, "I was unavoidably detained."

Jenny felt a laugh bubble up at his sheer audacity, but she forced it down. "And your purpose in coming today?"

"I wanted to ask if you'd go driving with me tomorrow afternoon."

Jenny blinked at the matter-of-fact answer. She peered more closely at his face, but there was nothing in his lapis eyes to indicate that he was less than sincere. Yet it was impossible to believe. "I confess to some confusion, sir. Perhaps you had better sit down."

Kevin obligingly settled himself on the sofa. She crossed to the wing-backed chair opposite him, and spread her skirts to sit before realizing that perhaps he had expected her to sit beside him.

Watching her, Kevin found himself feeling oddly nonplussed. When he had been ushered into the room and left to cool his heels, he had looked around himself with interest in hopes the room would tell him more about its owner. He had thought it had. The floor-to-ceiling, west-facing windows took up one entire wall and were draped in yards of filmy light-filtering white gauze with white-on-white satin panels held back on either side by gilded ivy tie backs. The wall opposite the door was hung in a similar satin in saffron shot with gold, with a white marble fireplace in the center. The painting over the fireplace was a sunny pastoral scene in a gilt frame. The other walls were painted the same light yellow and boasted other paintings and miniatures well spaced and nicely grouped. The furnishings consisted of the white satin sofa on which he reposed, two yellow wing-backed chairs opposite flanking the fireplace, several decorative tables on which perched figurines, vases of flowers, or other knickknacks, and three glass cabinets with similar items. All in all, it was a cheery, richly furnished, decidedly feminine room. And it seemed to fit the stern-faced woman in front of him not a bit.

The woman he fondly remembered from the fall dance had been tall and regal. The outmoded dress she wore had failed to conceal her womanly curves. He knew it had been the rumor that she was unattainable that had inspired him to ask her to dance, but in doing so he had caught a glimpse of a vulnerable, gentle lady that he had felt drawn to protect. Despite her unenthusiastic reception today, he felt the same feeling and realized ruefully that the person she most needed protection from was himself.

By sheer determination, he forced himself not to squirm under her direct gaze. Before she could speak, he decided to go on the attack.

"What is it you'd like me to clarify, Madam, to help alleviate this confusion you spoke of?"

Jenny hesitated. She had been studying him as closely as he had been studying her. What she saw confused her even more. As Fiching had surmised, this man was obviously a polished example of the breed Corinthian, a breed she usually went out of her way to avoid. Their frivolous, sensation-seeking, devil-may-care attitude repelled her, as it seemed the complete antithesis of her quiet way of life. Yet, hadn't she just been wishing for a change?

"Tell me, Mr. Whattling," she replied with determination. "What made you decide to seek me out now?"

Kevin decided to be as honest as possible. "When we stood up together at the Bamingers', there was something about you that made me think we should get better acquainted."

No doubt my brilliant conversation, Jenny thought wryly. Aloud she prompted, "Better acquainted?"

"Yes. There seemed to be a common purpose, a meeting of minds if you will, that made me feel we might be friends."

"Friends?" Jenny stared at him in amazement. It was the last thing she had expected him to say. "You thought we could be friends?"

He smiled. "Does that surprise you, Madam?"

"Surprise me? It shocks me to the core. I have a certain reputation, sir, as a bluestocking, while you are clearly a dyed-in-the-wool Corinthian. Are you sure you have the right person?"

He chuckled at her assessment. "Oh, you're the right person. I know of no rules that say a Corinthian and a bluestocking cannot enjoy each other's company. So, what say you, Madam? Will you come driving with me tomorrow?"

Jenny shook her head. It really was very ironic—here was the most handsome of princes, and she simply couldn't believe it. "I'm sorry sir, if I appear dense, but your, er, interest in building this friendship seems most precipitous. Without roundaboutation, if you will—why me, why now?"

His face grew solemn, making him look years older and not a little weary. "Very well, Madam, if you insist. I am grossly in debt and only a quick and advantageous marriage can keep me from the Poor House. I have been told I could have any woman in England. I'm sentimental enough to want to at least feel a little affection for the woman I marry. I've looked over the prospects carefully, and you were my first choice." His grin reappeared suddenly, blazing in its intensity. "In short, Miss Eugennia Welch, I intend to marry you."

He knew it was a bold statement, but the lady before him froze and stared at him, her hazel eyes wide, and he had a sudden sinking feeling that he had overplayed his hand. She recovered her composure with an obvious effort and rose to stride majestically to the door. Convention demanded that he rise as well, but he did so with a tremor. *That's it,* he thought. *She's tossing me out.* She threw open the door, and he tensed.

"Fiching, leave Mr. Whattling and me alone for a time, if you please," she said to the elderly butler, who had been standing beside the door looking surprisingly stunned for one whose profession required an impassive front. "Leave the door open and see that we are not disturbed. If I raise my voice, you are to come in immediately with Stevens and Jenkins."

He looked at her askance, then bowed before what he saw in her face. She turned back to Kevin.

Jenny paused and took a deep breath. The thought that Martha might have been right about making wishes flitted through her mind, but she put it forcefully aside. How extraordinarily disappointing! She must deal with him as she had the others who had insulted her by preferring the money to the woman. She had no interest in any of her servants hearing about it either. She knew she could trust Fiching to be discreet, telling no one except perhaps Martha. Clasping her hands behind her back in an effort to calm herself, she regarded Kevin and was surprised to see him look as upset as she felt.

"Mr. Whattling," she said firmly, "I appreciate your frankness. Let me be equally honest." She started to tell him that she had no interest in marrying, but found she could not bring the words to her lips, given her latest mood. She started to amend it to say that she had no interest in marrying *him*, but he was too uncannily like the vision of her handsome prince for that to be true either. She resorted to a fact she knew to be true. "We can have little in common. Why do you think we could possibly suit?"

The nervousness evaporated, and his enchanting grin reappeared. "Come driving with me and you might find out."

Despite her misgivings, she found herself returning his smile. "You are most tenacious, sir. But why, if I may be so bold, should I agree to this meeting if I do not see a happy end?"

"Do you gamble, Madam?" When she shook her head, he tried another direction. "Have you ever played whist?"

Did he think her so lacking in the social graces as that? Jenny wondered, suddenly hurt. "Everyone who is anyone plays whist, sir," she informed him icily.

"Of course. Forgive the question." He bowed. "I was merely trying to develop an analogy. When we play whist, we play it for the chance of beating a worthy opponent, of besting our own expectations. It is the *chance* that the game will be worth playing that encourages us to play. I am merely asking you to take that same chance."

She conceded his point with a nod. "But whist is an enjoyable pastime, I have always found. It sharpens the intellect. My experience with driving has not been so pleasurable."

His grin widened. "That, Madam, is because you've never been driving with me."

Jenny caught herself laughing. While she was still sure she could never bring herself to be courted by a fortune hunter, she found herself tempted to take him up on his offer of a drive. Driving with him might indeed be enjoyable, and it would definitely be different from her usual occupations.

"Very well, sir, I will drive with you tomorrow. However," she added quickly as he beamed in triumph, "I promise nothing more. Going driving in no way indicates that I will accept your offer of marriage."

He bowed. "I understand completely, Miss Welch. I shall try not to let your acceptance turn my head." The twinkle in his deep blue eyes belied the seriousness of his tone. "Will half past two in the afternoon be a suitable time?"

"Quite suitable," she agreed.

"Then I shall take my leave until then." He strode to her side, took her hand, and raised it to his lips. Looking down into her eyes, he held her hand, and her gaze, just longer than was proper, and Jenny swore she could feel the warmth of his touch travel from her gloved fingers through her entire body.

"Until tomorrow, Miss Welch," he murmured, bowing himself out.

Jenny stood where he had left her for some time, trying to sort through her conflicting feelings. She found his presence exhilarating, but his proposal audacious. As if she would ever give in to a proposal of marriage simply because the gentleman had a handsome face and a charming manner! She had righteously rejected the last three fortune hunters who had dared to propose. Her withdrawn lifestyle and reputation as a bluestocking had held off others who might otherwise have been tempted by her fortune to seek her out. So even if he had been more charming than the others, why should she encourage him?

Perhaps because she had been wishing so fervently for a change. Well, she had certainly gotten her wish. Her handsome prince had appeared and proposed, and instead of romance, she felt—what? Disappointment that if he were sincere he hadn't sought her out sooner. Anger that what he apparently really wanted was her money. Chagrin that she hadn't been able to react more appropriately to his advances, though truthfully, she wasn't sure how a fashionable young miss was supposed to react to such an audacious proposal. Perhaps she should have slapped his face. But he had been so utterly charming about the whole affair. And when she thought about driving with him on the morrow, well, the truth was, she was scared to death.

A cough roused her from her thoughts, and she turned to see Fiching and Miss Tindale both peering in the open doorway.

"Did you accept him, miss?" the butler asked hopefully.

"Did you send him packing?" Martha sniffed with equal hope.

"Neither," Jenny replied with a toss of her head. She walked past them to the stairs. "We are going driving tomorrow." As she climbed to the second floor, she wondered if twenty-four hours would be enough time to choose a suitable outfit.

Four

It was a bemused Kevin who agreed to Giles and Nigel's suggestion that they have dinner at White's. He went as their guest of course. In the first place, he hadn't the funds, and in the second, he had resigned his membership after Robbie's death. Besides, they were careful to keep him away from Watier's these days, where the wildest gaming was to be had. Both Nigel and Giles tried to pretend nothing was untoward, dressing in their usual evening black even as he did. But they exchanged looks of concern when he glanced at some of the gentlemen already engaged in cards. He turned his attention to the dandies at the bow windows instead.

His friends needn't have worried, he reflected as they led him to a table well away from the others. He had no intention of going near a card table for the rest of his life, and he had little interest in gambling. Moreover, he hadn't been able to bring himself to go near Gentleman Jackson's to box more than once a week since Robbie's death. He knew Nigel and Giles feared his sudden change of behavior was because of his lack of funds. He knew it went far deeper. Even with Miss Welch's fortune at his fingertips, he wasn't going to be tempted again. He was through with gambling, and the next time he expected to go near a boxing match was when he taught his own sons a few tricks.

If he ever had sons. He wondered whether Miss Welch wanted children. It probably didn't matter if she didn't. He hadn't the luxury of caring. But he had always wanted children, daughters as well as sons. His memories of his childhood were somewhat empty until his mother had re-married and had Robbie. Although there had been seven years between them, he had always loved his brother. He hoped that when he married, his children would be similarly pleased with each other.

Then again, he had always thought that when he eventually married it would be to some girl who adored him. He wasn't sure whether he would get to that point with Miss Welch. Those hazel eyes of hers were oddly innocent and knowing at the same time. If he understood her reactions, she wasn't sure she ought to be seen with him, but felt awfully tempted to do so. It was a temptation he could play on. Indeed, it was his strongest card at the moment. He didn't have much else to commend himself.

And she was going to be a much more difficult woman to woo than he had originally thought. While he had heard she tended to avoid Society, he had thought it only a story manufactured by those who were jealous of her intelligence. However, if today's conversation was any indication, she was not only antisocial, but more suspicious than he had expected of his motives. He would have to go carefully.

Still, it was hard not to be confident of victory. He was a far better deal than she was likely to get otherwise. While he had no doubt that she had been courted by fortune hunters before, at least he was honest about it. If she wasn't quite the woman he had expected she would be, she was still a taking little thing, and he was sure he would grow even fonder of her with time. Having a wife would certainly give him something to focus on beyond his own difficulties. He would be able to pay the last of his debts and still live well. All in all, it hadn't been a bad start.

Nigel wasn't willing to agree. "But did she say she would look favorably on your suit, old man?" he demanded over their mutton and Yorkshire pudding after Kevin had made his sketchy report of his afternoon's call.

"What woman ever immediately agrees to your suit, Nigel?" Kevin replied disparagingly.

"None," Giles sighed. "Although I had been hoping you might be different, Kev."

Kevin smiled. "I can only say that Miss Welch is much more discriminating than some. But then, I'm a much better catch than some."

"And your need is greater," Giles nodded. Nigel frowned at him, and he paled. "Er, no offense meant."

"None taken. Gentlemen, let us have no secrets in this regard. I want you as my knee and bottlemen for this bout. In other words, I can only win Miss Welch with your help. In fact, I already have a favor to ask. Nigel, if I'm to take Miss Welch driving tomorrow, I shall need a carriage."

"Done," Nigel nodded, taking a bite of his mutton. "Take the curricle. It only has two seats. She'll have to leave her maid at home."

"Oh, I say," Giles puffed, but Kevin wasn't sure whether it was in protest or admiration.

Kevin approved the idea. "Good suggestion. And I don't suppose you'd part with the whites?"

Nigel chewed his lower lip for a moment. "You've given up racing as well, I'm sure."

Kevin met his look straight on. "You know I have. I'll take good care of your horses, Nigel. I promise."

Nigel nodded. "Very well then. The whites and the curricle. Do you want my tiger as well?"

Kevin grinned. "If you can spare your servant. And your new tweed greatcoat."

Nigel grumbled something under cover of forking in another mouthful.

"You're welcome to my greatcoat, Kev," Giles offered.

"Thanks, old man, but we aren't exactly the same size. As it is, I'll have to go easy not to rip the seams in Nigel's, and I'd better leave it open so she won't notice it's too short for me. Nigel, I'll come by after twelve to get them, if that's all right. I'm to pick her up at half past two."

Nigel shook his head. "Driving with Eugennia Welch. What do you bet the conversation will be nothing but scholarly quotes and ponderous posturing?"

Kevin chuckled. "At the very least, I'd wager she won't remark on my horses, the weather, or the fold of my cravat."

"I'll take that wager," Nigel grinned.

"So will I," a deep voice put in. Nigel's face froze into his milk-curdling frown. Giles turned as white as milk. Recognizing the voice, Kevin understood why.

"Take yourself off, Safton," he murmured without turning to look at the man behind him. "This is a private party."

"But Whattling, I wasn't aware you were up to attending parties yet. My apologies for not checking on you sooner. When you're finished with these good gentlemen, come locate me. I'm sure we can find more interesting sport."

"Mr. Whattling doesn't play cards anymore," Nigel growled. "Nor is he interested in any other activity you might care to mention."

George Safton moved to stand beside the table. Kevin refused to look up at him. He didn't need to see the face to be reminded of the nearly black eyes that glittered with malice as easily as amusement, or the thin lips that twisted into cruelty as easily as cunning. At nine o'clock in the evening, George Safton would be dressed in spotless black evening wear that would make the women raise their quizzing glasses and comment on how his black hair shone as brightly as the head of his ebony walking stick. Kevin knew that by daybreak, the cutaway coat and knee breeches would be soiled with spilled wine and stink of stale smoke. The creamy white cravat would be wrinkled and gray with sweat. And on at least one night, the black and white striped waistcoat would be spotted with blood. No, he didn't need to look at George Safton to know him for what he was. He only wished he had seen it sooner.

"Why, Dillingham," George purred beside them, "have you managed to change him into a mewling lamb at last? How very sad. Robbie would be so disappointed."

Kevin surged to his feet, blood roaring in his ears. "Don't you ever mention that name in my presence again! The magistrates may not have enough evidence to convict you, but we all know your involvement in my brother's death. Be glad I don't call you out. Now get out of my sight before I forget myself!"

Nigel and Giles had risen as well, Nigel putting a hand on Kevin's arm and all of Giles's bulk trembling with suppressed emotion. Their fellows at the surrounding tables exchanged looks or raised their eyebrows. Safton didn't so much as glance at them. "No need to get hostile, my good man. I meant no harm. You know I had the utmost respect for your brother. I feel his loss as well."

"If you feel anything," Kevin said quietly, "it's the loss of your easiest victim. I'm not my brother. Leave me alone."

Safton shrugged. "Very well. I tried. For Robbie's sake, I tried. You leave me no choice but to remind you that I hold vouchers of your brother's amounting to over two thousand pounds. I'd like to know when I shall be paid."

Kevin resumed his seat, long fingers tearing at his Yorkshire pudding. "You'll be paid as soon as I can raise your blood money. I assure you, it won't be soon enough for me."

"That's all I wanted to hear." He offered Giles and Nigel a bow. "Gentlemen." Only Nigel watched his retreating back.

"Odious muckworm," Giles sputtered. "How you ever came to be involved with him, Kev, is more than I'll ever know."

"Cut line, Sloane," Nigel barked. "We all know how charming Safton can be when trying to lure someone in. First Kevin, then Robbie. Kevin was lucky to get out."

"Unlike Robbie," Kevin murmured.

Nigel resumed his seat as well and, after a moment, Giles joined him. "Perhaps we should find another club," Nigel grumbled, poking at his mutton, which was now obviously cold. "They seem to be letting anyone in White's these days."

"You'll have to go pretty far to avoid him," Giles provided helpfully. "I don't understand why, but he is widely received."

"That's because he always manages to let someone else take the blame," Kevin explained, poking at his own meal. "It would give me great pleasure to see him caught. But right now, I haven't that luxury either."

"Here now, none of that," Nigel ordered. "We have a campaign to plan. You are taking Miss Welch driving tomorrow. That is only the start. We need to lay out a plan of attack. I will brook no further interruptions."

Kevin shook his head, rising. He suddenly had no interest in anything but his own company. "No, thank you, gentlemen. I think I've had enough for one night. Be assured that as soon as I know what I want to do about Miss Welch, you will be the first to know."

Eugennia also found herself discussing Kevin's unexpected visit with a friend. As she had predicted earlier, Miss Susan St. John came calling later that afternoon to speak about their next reading project. Jenny and Miss Tindale received her in the library, a lofty-ceilinged room lined with oak bookshelves, with chairs scattered about on the Aubusson carpets in pools of sunlight from the south-facing windows.

"I know you have your heart set on *Mansfield Park,*" she said in the straightforward manner that had won Jenny's respect from the first. "But I think we should start the books by this 'lady of quality' with the first, which was *Sense and Sensibility.*"

Miss Tindale nodded agreeably. Jenny couldn't seem to find a logical reason to disagree, though it seemed to her that she'd had a flawless argument on the subject earlier. "Very well, if you feel strongly."

"And we should increase our pace a bit," Susan added, patting down the skirts of her green-sprigged muslin dress. "It took us nearly a month to read Scott's *Waverly*. If we are to keep up with all the new literature coming out these days, we must do better than that. I think we should try to do *Sense and Sensibility* in ten days' time."

Miss Tindale nodded again. Eugennia was going through the content of her wardrobe in her mind. The brown poplin was far too maidenly, but she didn't own anything that could be called daring. "Yes," she murmured, "that would be fine."

"And I promised Lord Davies you'd donate your Egyptian collection to be viewed with the Elgin marbles."

Miss Tindale's mouth dropped open, gray eyes wide in shock.

"How nice," Jenny nodded, thinking that her navy kerseymere was too dark, but her gray lustring was too light.

Susan scowled, her light green eyes streaks of bright jade against the alabaster of her skin and the midnight of her face-framing ringlets inside her straw bonnet. "I knew it!" she declared. "You haven't been listening to a word I've said. I suppose you've settled on a new course of study. We may as well discuss that instead, for you'll be useless on any other subject until it has run its course."

Jenny offered her a contrite smile. "I'm sorry, Susan. I seem to be easily distracted today. By all means, let us discuss the reading circle. I promise to pay closer attention."

"But what is distracting you?" Susan demanded.

Miss Tindale sniffed, looking smug. "A gentleman."

While Susan raised her fine dark eyebrows, Jenny frowned at Martha. "Hardly a gentleman. It is nothing, Susan. Pray continue."

"Nothing, eh?" Susan replied, glancing between Martha, who had the good sense to pale under Jenny's glare, and Jenny, who was blushing. "Nothing you care to discuss with your closest friend?"

Jenny attempted to meet her light gaze straight on, but found herself studying the nearest bookcase instead. "You will only scold me for being foolish."

"Eugennia Welch, a fool?" Susan looked astonished. "You know I would never think such a ridiculous thing. What have you done?"

"You may as well tell all," Martha advised knowingly. "You can be sure she will not stop until you do."

Jenny sighed. "Very well. A gentleman did come calling

today, Susan. He asked me to drive tomorrow, and I accepted. That's really all there is to it."

"That is a farradiddle," Susan declared. "Miss Tindale is picking at her bombazine, so I know you are evading an issue. What is it? Was he ugly? Is that why you fear to tell me?"

Miss Tindale snorted. "Ugly is hardly the word for him."

Susan raised both eyebrows. "Fat as well? Eugennia, he must be brilliant for you to agree to drive with him."

Jenny caught herself smiling. "He is sufficiently impressive."

"I cannot sit here and listen to you praise him," Miss Tindale cried. "Miss St. John, surely you can get her to see reason. The man is a cad, a fortune hunter. He so much as asked her to marry him, on the first acquaintance!"

"That is enough, Martha," Eugennia told her sternly. "You know I value your advice, but I must do as I see fit, especially in matters pertaining to the heart."

"The heart!" Martha leaped to her feet. "Do you hear that, Miss St. John? She admits he has engaged her heart. This is far more serious than I thought. Eugennia, you must stop this!"

Jenny reached out a hand and tugged her back into her seat. "Now, Martha, calm yourself. I spoke without thinking."

"An indicator in itself," Susan put in. "Perhaps you ought to tell me everything. To start with, what is this gentleman's name?"

"Kevin Whattling," Jenny replied. "You remember him, Susan. He was the very tall gentleman who asked me to dance at the Bamingers' ball during the Little Season."

Susan blinked. "The splendid Corinthian? The one with the engaging smile?"

"The very one," Jenny smiled. "I knew you would remember. He is apparently deep in debt and looking for a wealthy wife. I have no intention of accepting his offer, but I thought a drive might be diverting."

"Diverting will hardly be the word for it," Susan predicted. "Jenny, you must promise me to take Miss Tindale with you."

Now Jenny blinked even as Martha preened. "Well, certainly, but why are you so adamant?"

"My dear, you and I have had little experience with such gentlemen, although I have certainly heard a great deal from my three sisters, who as you know are incorrigible flirts. Perhaps I can put this more logically. In the taxonomy of the animal kingdom, there are predators and prey. I'm very afraid, my dear, that your Mr. Whattling is the predator. I don't think I have to tell you where that places you."

"Thank God, someone with sense," Martha sighed. "Please, Jenny, listen to her. When he comes tomorrow, tell him you've made a mistake."

Jenny glanced between their concerned faces. Martha was overprotective, but she had never known her to be so outspoken on an issue. Susan's intelligence and good advice were unquestionable. Was she making a mistake? Should she have refused his offer of a drive? She could easily have Fiching tell the gentleman that she was indisposed; then she could simply refuse to be home to him in the future. It wasn't as if she had to even see him again, if she didn't want to.

She smiled at both of them. "Thank you both for your care. I will think about what you have said. In fact, I doubt I will think of much else."

Martha relaxed. "Good. Then we can have Fiching tell the fellow to whistle."

"No," Jenny replied, and Martha and Susan both started. "I said I would think on what you said, and I shall. However, I shall also honor my promise to drive with Mr. Whattling tomorrow. There isn't anything you can say to stop me, so we may as well choose another subject for discussion. I do not wish to hear another word on the subject of Mr. Kevin Whattling."

Five

As Eugennia had expected, twenty-four hours had indeed been a lamentably short time in which to prepare oneself to drive through Hyde Park with a handsome prince. Miss Tindale could not be convinced that such an outing was not the revenge of the gods, but she reluctantly agreed to help a concerned Eugennia find the right attire. However, as Eugennia deplored the shopping and fittings and primping necessary to maintain a stylish wardrobe, there was precious little from which to choose. Her best gowns were those purchased for evening wear, which were totally unsuited for a drive through the park. Her day dresses were as a rule dark, perfect for a literary debate with her circle, but much too solemn for an outing such as this. In the end, she selected a dove-colored, silk morning dress with a matching pelisse trimmed in triple rows of black braid on the neck, sleeves, and hem. When Miss Tindale settled the black chip hat on her braided hair, Eugennia scowled at the picture she presented in her mirror.

"I look like the sour-faced old maid they all expect me to be," she complained.

Martha stepped back, looking hurt. "It's the best of the lot. Although I still don't see why you must go through with this, perhaps Mr. Whattling's attentions will convince you to visit that modiste Miss St. John recommended to you the other day."

Eugennia rose and shook out her skirts as if that would banish her nervousness. "Modiste indeed. I haven't even gone on this silly drive and already you want me to act like a simpering debutante." She put out her chin and squared her shoulders. "If Mr. Whattling is sincere in his attentions, he'll take me as I am." So saying, she strolled confidently out the door and down the corridor.

She hadn't even reached the stairs before her bloom of confidence withered. It was all very well and good to stand up to Miss Tindale and Susan; it was harder to convince herself. In truth, she had spent much of the night regretting her impulsive decision in agreeing to this meeting. She saw nothing interesting in moving at a crawl through crowded Hyde Park, jerking one's horses to a stop every few minutes to nod to someone one scarcely knew or cared about. She always felt as if her brain atrophied at such events. And she didn't much care for the gossip that she knew she caused with her infrequent attendance at these social gatherings. Whatever had she been thinking of to agree to go today?

She reached the head of the stairs and saw Fiching on his way up. Below him in the entry hall, Kevin grinned at her. His tan tweed greatcoat made his hair appear golden. Through the coat's opening, she could see his chamois breeches hugged his powerful legs. His eyes, so much like the lapis in the stones she had purchased from the Egyptologist, would hold that telltale twinkle, she had no doubt. She swallowed and pasted a smile on her face. When a handsome prince beckoned, what could she do but respond?

Kevin raised her hand to his lips as she reached the bottom of the stairs, and she almost faltered. She swore her stomach flipped over, even though she knew that to be anatomically impossible. He solemnly presented her with a nosegay of violets and tiny yellow tea roses, and she lowered her head in the pretense of smelling them while she tried to regain her composure.

"Punctual as well as intelligent," Kevin smiled down at her. "You put half the women in London to shame." He tucked her arm in his and led her to the door.

Martha was sputtering at the head of the stairs, but Eugennia wasn't sure she wanted to know whether her hair was out of place or her coat had a string loose. Fiching cleared his throat, and she frowned at him.

"I regret that the curricle only has room for two," Kevin murmured beside her. "But we will be out in public, so you need have no fear for your reputation."

Behind him, Fiching was nodding his head vigorously. Eugennia didn't need to look at Miss Tindale behind her to know that Martha would be scowling. This was what Susan had warned her about. He was using his charm to manipulate her into doing something she knew wasn't exactly right. She glanced up at that potent smile and eyes one could drown in. It was working.

She found herself smiling up at him. "Martha, we'll talk when I return. I'm sure I can count on Mr. Whattling to behave as a gentleman."

His smile was anything but gentlemanly. "I promise to be on my best behavior, Miss Welch."

She handed Fiching the flowers and ignored his grin of triumph as Kevin led her out the door.

It didn't take longer for Eugennia's confidence to plummet once more than the walk to the neat white curricle with gold-rimmed wheels that stood waiting. She realized she should keep the conversation flowing and struggled to find something to say as he handed her up. Unfortunately, the touch of his hand on her arm sent fresh tremors through her body and seemed to drive any thought of intelligent conversation completely out of her mind. As he jumped up beside her, she looked ahead, and her glance fell on the pair of horses who drew the carriage. While she was no judge of horseflesh, she could see they were perfectly matched and as white as the enameled paneling of the carriage.

"What lovely horses," she ventured.

To her complete dismay, Kevin burst into laughter.

"I'm sorry, Miss Welch," he chuckled as the tiger who had been holding the horses jumped to the back of the carriage. Kevin snapped the reins. "I had a conversation last night with the friend from whom I borrowed this rig, and I wagered him that a woman of your intellect would not discuss the weather, my cravat, or my horses. I stand corrected."

Eugennia colored in a blush. "It was my understanding," she replied defensively, "that you Corinthians did not feel the day complete unless someone had admired your horses."

"Ah, but these are not my horses."

"Well, really, sir, there was no need to borrow others. While these are lovely beasts, I'm sure yours would have been fine."

His smile froze, and he turned to watch the road. "I have no horses, Miss Welch. I was forced to sell my stables to pay my living expenses."

Eugennia focused on the road as well, fighting back tears. No matter what she did or said, she made a fool of herself. She should have stayed home. With this auspicious beginning, they trundled into Hyde Park.

The day was balmy for London in early March, and the main paths through the park were thronged with carriages, riders, and pedestrians enjoying the early spring sun. It was, if anything, even more crowded than Eugennia had feared. Kevin was forced to slow the horses to an amble, while he was greeted time and again by others intent on traversing the park in a like manner. Most were content to wave or call his name, and so Eugennia was spared the necessity of having to find suitable topics of conversation. Several, however, attempted closer contact, and she soon began to fear Martha's warning that her face would indeed freeze in this pointlessly polite smile.

Kevin found himself enjoying the ride far less than he had expected. True, he hadn't driven through the park since Robbie's death, but he didn't remember it being so damnably crowded. What he really wanted to do was spend time conversing with Miss Welch, but every few moments someone else interrupted. He had no idea he was known to so many people, or that all of them had decided to go riding or driving in Hyde Park at half-past two in the afternoon on a Friday. He was beginning to lose patience with the whole process and tried to think of a plausible excuse for leaving so soon. Miss Welch would surely think him inconstant if he simply took her home early. In fact, she had been growing more quiet with each interruption. Glancing over at her, he saw that her round face was pale, her generous mouth compressed into a thin line. She obviously was having as poor a time as he was. Surely there was somewhere else he could drive her where they could be alone.

He glanced ahead again, calculating the distance through the trees to where the park opened near Upper Grosvenor. There were a good number of carriages and riders between him and freedom, but if he pushed it a bit, he should be able to make it in a quarter hour. He started to encourage the horses forward when he noticed the two riders they were passing on the left. Both were trying diligently to admire the scenery, pretending somehow that their red riding jackets blended in with the green of the park.

It was Nigel and Giles.

He scowled at them and had the satisfaction of seeing Giles whiten. Nigel scowled back. He had a sudden urge to whip the horses, but refused to mistreat animals just to get even with interfering gentlemen, however well meaning. Friends or no friends, he vowed, he refused to acknowledge the busybodies. At least, not while Miss Welch was at his side. He ignored them, determined more than ever to leave the park.

He was so focused on reaching Upper Grovesnor that Eugennia had to clear her throat twice before he realized he had been addressed. Turning, he saw the occupant of the open carriage they were passing on the right. The fine-shaped face was paler than usual, her large lower lip made larger in decided annoyance. The fashionable feathered bonnet failed to hide the dark profusion of curls or the long pointed nose. Eugennia wasn't sure who the lady was in the wine-colored coach, but she felt herself tense looking into the deep-set dark eyes that seemed to be regarding her sharply.

"Kevin Whattling," the woman snapped. "Has your mourning made you deaf, sir? Or is it that you have forsaken polite company too long that you refuse to answer a lady's call?"

Kevin inclined his head in a bow. "Countess Lieven, a pleasure as always. My only excuse for my rudeness is that I find it difficult to concentrate with so much beauty so near."

As his smile indicated that he was obviously including Eugennia in the statement, she caught herself blushing.

The countess flashed him a tight smile. "I see you have recovered your usual charm. I can only say that it is about time you put that nonsense with Mr. Safton behind you. Mr. Greene's death was a tragic accident; ruining your own life in atonement would have been far worse."

Eugennia could feel Kevin tense beside her. But before he could answer, or she could puzzle over the words, the countess's eyes met her own.

"And Miss Welch, isn't it? How nice to see you out as well. The spring sunshine does wonders for the spirit, does it not? You must bring her by Almack's some night, Mr. Whattling. I'll send round a voucher." With a nod, she signaled to her driver to move on.

"Almack's," Eugennia breathed, stunned. She hadn't received a card for that hallowed establishment even when she had come out eight years ago. While her lineage was impeccable, she had never had the dash to commend herself to any of the patronesses. Yet one drive with Kevin Whattling had changed all that. She gazed at her companion with amazement.

Kevin brought himself under control with an effort. Surely there would come a time when the mere mention of his brother would fail to bring the memories crashing in on him. He had to regain control of himself. He managed to turn to Eugennia with a smile.

"I shall be delighted to escort you to Almack's any night you choose, Miss Welch," he assured her, noting that she was gazing at him in a manner that left him strangely self-conscious. He focused instead on directing the horses around a large barouche that was blocking the way. Two carriages down, half a dozen left to go before he made it out of the park. Unfortunately, partially past the latest carriage, another female voice called his name.

"Mr. Kevin Whattling! Mr. Whattling! I am most vexed with you!"

Recognizing the voice, he smothered a groan as he pulled the horses to a stop again. He shook his head at Eugennia's puzzled frown. "Forgive me, Miss Welch. Duty calls. I shall try to be quick about it." He turned to face the two well-dressed young women who reposed in the open carriage.

"Miss Tate, Miss Ashley, how nice to see you."

Miss Tate, a titian-haired beauty with large green eyes, pouted prettily. Eugennia, who could not imagine her mouth taking on so enchanting a shape when vexed, hated her on sight.

"Really, Mr. Whattling, it is simply too dreadful of you to greet us so cheerfully when you failed to appear at our ball last night."

"Absolutely dreadful," chimed in Miss Ashley, a buxom blonde.

"Ladies, my most abject apologies. The Regent had me to Carlton House, and I simply couldn't escape. Duty, you know, is a harsh mistress. Much harsher a mistress than most of the charming ladies of my acquaintance."

The ladies in question tittered appreciatively.

Eugennia felt ill.

"But ladies," Kevin continued to her sudden dismay. "Let me make you known to my delightful companion. Miss Eugennia Welch, may I present Miss Sylvia Tate and Miss Aramide Ashley."

Eugennia murmured a polite greeting, and the two debutantes responded with similar lack of enthusiasm.

"Let us not keep you," Kevin said smoothly. He continued to push the horses until they were safely past the barouche. Eugennia had no doubt that if she were to look back, she would find the women whispering behind their hands.

"You do that disgustingly well," she sighed with a certain amount of envy.

"What? Drive the carriage?"

"No, conversing with near strangers. You do it so well. I can never think of anything to say."

She looked so sincerely downcast that Kevin was amazed. "You? Miss Welch, you astonish me. I have it on good authority that you are a well-read, well-educated, witty woman. Why on earth should you feel tongue-tied?"

"Perhaps precisely because I am well read and well educated. They"—she waved to indicate everyone else in the park—"I fear, are not."

"Do you think yourself their better, then?" Kevin asked, still confused.

"Good heavens, no! In their eyes, they are far superior." When he looked further shocked by her statement, she continued on determinedly. "You needn't be charming about it, Mr. Whattling. I know what the ton thinks of me. I'm different, I'm odd. I'm the bluestocking, the spinster, the old maid who actually dares to prefer her dusty old books to their glittering society. What am I to say to them?"

"Why, say anything you like. If they don't like it, tell them to go hang."

She laughed despite herself. "That would surely improve my standing."

"Is that what you want? To make yourself better in their eyes? I say, be yourself first, Madam. Anyone who can't appreciate that is beneath your notice."

Eugennia stared at him in astonishment. "Why, Mr. Whattling, that was absolutely eloquent!"

He grinned. "Not bad for an ill-read, poorly educated Corinthian, eh?" He looked back at the horses to maneuver them around two more slowly moving equipages, still intent on reaching the exit. He glanced back over his shoulder to make sure no one else was trying to pass on the left. Behind three carriages and two knots of riders, George Safton was urging his stallion toward them. Kevin whirled forward.

"Blast. Hang on, Miss Welch. I'll try to lose him."

"Who?" Eugennia began, then was forced to grab the edge of the leather seat as Kevin attempted to pass a group of riders ahead of them. Even as he pulled around, there was a sudden pounding of hooves and a hail from behind. She glanced back and caught a glimpse of a raven-haired man on a large, powerful, mean-looking black horse. Glancing back at her companion, she saw his lovely mouth set in a determined line.

"You were quite right, Miss Welch," he clipped. "Driving in Hyde Park is a disgusting pursuit. I much prefer country air." He whipped up the horses and careened out of the park before Eugennia could gasp in agreement.

Six

Eugennia sat silently in the curricle as Kevin swiftly passed the London traffic and headed on the Old North Road away from the city. Around them, houses were giving way to pastures and hedgerows. Curricles and lorries became farm carts and traveling coaches. She ought to feel frightened, she thought, as he took her farther and farther from civilization. If he were going to take her to a secluded inn to compromise her and force her to marry him, this headlong flight was a good start. However, stealing a glance at his face, eyes narrowed unseeingly at the road ahead, she was somehow sure that she was in no danger from his attentions. It was far more likely that he'd send the carriage into a ditch with his careless driving.

Something had obviously upset him, starting with Countess Lieven's mention of the death of a Mr. Greene. Her natural curiosity flared. What had the late Mr. Greene to do with a charming fortune hunter? Any analysis would be premature, as she had very few facts about that situation. Indeed, she had very few facts about Mr. Kevin Whattling himself. She knew that he was greatly in debt, although she did not think he had mentioned the exact amount. His fashionable clothes and polished style bespoke the Corinthian; he had admitted he considered himself such. Yet he conversed with a great deal more depth than any of the Corinthians it had been her misfortune to meet. There were moments, such as during their drive through the park, when she was sure he had a great refinement of spirit. On the other hand, his easy way with the ladies said that he had probably never had his heart broken. It was quite possible all his lapses into serious conversation had merely been a ruse. He certainly tried to pretend that aside from his debts, he hadn't a care in the world. Given his mood, that, at least, was obviously a lie.

So, who was Mr. Whattling? she wondered, studying his profile. That thoughtful brow was at odds with the pointed chin, she decided, as if he were a philosopher and a sprite at once. One moment he was Hamlet the brooding prince, the next Puck the trickster. Neither had met with happy ends, she knew. Would it be wise to come to know him better, or should she finish this drive and send him on his way?

She had so many questions, and of course she could not ask him any of them without seeming as if she were prying. When he had whipped the reins for the third time in as many minutes, however, she decided she should try to break through the black mood that had apparently taken hold of him.

"I quite agree with you, Mr. Whattling," she began as if nothing untoward had happened, "that the country is a far nicer place for a drive than the city. However, I do believe we could enjoy it more if we could actually see it."

Kevin shook himself as if awakening from a dream. Indeed, his thoughts had been focused on a night three months ago that still seemed more nightmare than reality. There were moments when he could smell the stench of tobacco as it swirled in noxious clouds around the lamplight; hear the shouts of the crowd cheering for the Giant of Lancaster, who cast a darker shadow over Robbie, outmatching him in weight as well as reach. The one flash of brightness in the night was the gold in George Safton's hand that rose in triumph, even as Kevin heard the unmistakable crack of bone hitting bone. He shook himself again and the nightmare faded, showing him only the whites, bright in the early spring sunlight.

He obligingly slowed the lathered horses, but turning to his companion was harder. She must think him mad. There were times when he thought so himself. He had to find a plausible excuse for his actions.

"Forgive me, Miss Welch," he told her with a rueful smile. "I fear I was giving entirely too much attention to the horses."

Eugennia decided not to say what she thought of his obvious falsehood. It seemed far more important to bring back the charmer who had asked to take her driving. She had had entirely enough of Hamlet for one afternoon.

"And such lovely horses they are, too," she replied brightly in a near perfect imitation of Miss Tate's dewy manner. To complete the picture, she batted her eyes at him, tilting her face to the side in a picture of innocence.

Kevin chuckled, willing to let her be amusing. "Touché, Miss Welch. Yes, they are magnificent horses, and my cravat is tied in the most interesting fold, and the weather is most balmy for this time of year to be sure."

"Oh!" Eugennia raised her gloved hand to her mouth in mock dismay. "You've just used all three topics of conversation available to us. What can we possibly say to each other on the drive back?"

Kevin grinned saucily. "I'm sure we shall contrive. Shall I tell you how much I admire you?"

Eugennia shook her head. "I sincerely hope you can make better conversation than that, sir."

"Very well," Kevin grinned, "then shall I tell you how lovely you look in the sunshine?"

Eugennia rolled her eyes. "Oh, please. That should take all of ten seconds."

"Nonsense!" He looked offended. "I'll have you know I could rhapsodize about your nose alone for at least a quarter hour."

"My nose?" Eugennia frowned, touching the member with the tip of her finger to see if it had suddenly changed shape. "You cannot be serious, sir."

"Madam, when I am flirting I am always serious."

"But my nose?"

Kevin eyed her. "A quarter hour, I say. What are you willing to wager, my lady, that I can do it?"

Eugennia suddenly began to feel uneasy with the way the conversation was going. Charm was one thing, wagering was something else entirely. She shifted in her seat and pretended to admire the scenery. "Don't be ridiculous. Why would I take so foolish a chance?"

"Because the outcome would be vastly entertaining. Come now, Miss Welch, where is your spirit of adventure? We needn't wager for money, you know. A kiss would do nicely."

"Really, sir, you are too bold."

"Very well, the honor of escorting you to Almack's."

She peered at him cautiously, but he was grinning at her and it was impossible not to smile back. "Not much of an honor, sir," she informed him. "I doubt I will ever set foot in the place, voucher or no voucher."

"What!" He found it hard to believe she had never visited the place; every debutante he had ever met would have carried a cartload of coal to Newcastle if it would have brought a nod of approval from the famous patronesses. Even if she had somehow escaped their notice, she must surely wonder about the place. "Aren't you even curious what happens in those hallowed halls?"

He was teasing she knew, but she felt compelled to explain to him. "Curious, perhaps, but not enough to want to endure an evening of being stared at, gossiped about, and shunned by Society's best."

"I can assure you that would hardly be the case," he protested, feeling compelled to dispel these notions she had of the ton.

"And I can assure you that it would."

"You do have a truly dismal opinion of the rest of society, Miss Welch," he sighed, and she realized with surprise that she had truly saddened him. "I can only hope you will come to exclude me from that assessment."

"I have already excluded you, sir. Your chivalrous attention in the park was most kind, especially considering you are only courting me for my money."

"What!" Kevin pulled the horses up sharply, and Eugennia once more clutched the edge of the curricle trying to keep her seat. He maneuvered the horses to the side of the road, stopping the carriage, and turned to her. She recoiled before the intensity of his gaze.

"Madam, you do neither of us any credit by believing that. Obviously I have not made myself clear." He took hold of her shoulders, his mouth stern. How could she think she was worth no more than her fortune? After all, he was the one selling himself for a mess of porridge. If his attentions had managed to convince her of the reverse, he had indeed done her a disservice. He had to make her understand.

"I am courting you," he started, "because I think we might suit." He thought she might try to break his hold, but Eugennia could not have looked away if she tried. "You are a lovely woman, and it is my honor to escort you. It is an even greater honor that you would even consider my offer. The fact that you bring with you a considerable fortune is an added benefit, for I need it badly. However, if I find that we do not suit, or if you decide I am unworthy, I will find another heiress to wed."

Eugennia continued to stare at him, noting how his eyes darkened with emotion. Instead of lapis, she would have said cobalt. The gold of his lashes was reflected in the depths, and if she looked even deeper, she could see her own face regarding her back. She was looking at him so intently that Kevin found himself suddenly embarrassed by his outburst. He dropped his hold and sat back, straightening his coat. Then he picked up the reins and clucked to the horses.

"I should get you home," he murmured, turning them back toward town.

Eugennia faced forward again, feeling as if she had come through some sort of physical trial. Once again, he had been most eloquent, but this time she found it hard to believe he was sincere. If he was attracted to her to the point of courting, why had he waited until now to start? The most logical answer was, of course, because now he found himself in need of funds. It was hard to believe there was any other answer.

And would he really leave her be if he found they didn't suit? Logic told her that he wouldn't find many heiresses with her fortune, or, she amended ruefully, with her inexperience in social matters. She tried to remember who else Martha had said was still on the market. Evalina Turnpeth? But she generally spent the winter and spring in the Lake District. Fanny Brighton, perhaps, unless of course she had accepted that duke Jenny had sent packing. How many others were there with lesser fortunes? She somehow had never considered herself such a commodity.

And what was she to do if she was? Here again her knowledge of social requirements was woefully thin. Didn't gentlemen generally expect the lady they were courting to be interesting and pleasant to look upon? What if she hadn't been sufficiently interesting on this outing? What if he thought her taste in clothes atrocious? She glanced down at the black braid again and then up at his profile. He continued to watch the road ahead of them, but the tight lines of his face told her his thoughts had not lightened. What exactly was she supposed to do now?

It wasn't as easy to think of something bantering to say, she found to her dismay, when she felt she had something at stake. She caught herself wishing she had paid more attention to the governesses her father had paid to tutor her in the social arts. It had always seemed like such folderol, simpering and gushing over a gentleman just to make sure he called again, even when the first call had been boring beyond tears.

"It doesn't matter if you don't particularly enjoy a gentleman's company," she remembered one woman remarking, right before her father had let her go, "as long as the gentleman keeps coming back. One never knows: he may have a friend, or a cousin, who will be infinitely more interesting."

Then as now, the sentiment seemed highly mercenary to her. But of course, Kevin Whattling was hardly an unwanted caller. She had no need to keep him dangling like a worm on a hook to lure in other suitors. She was almost ashamed to admit it, but after only one drive, the only suitor she wanted was Kevin himself. With his mercurial moods and witty conversation, he was already infinitely interesting to her. The question was, was her fortune, and her meager social skills, enough to keep him interested in return?

She had been considering the matter for some time when she became aware that they were moving back into the city. Houses and businesses crowded on either side; carriages, lorries, riders, and pedestrians thronged the streets. Kevin would return her to her home soon, and the drive would be over.

She felt a sudden constriction in her throat and cast another sidelong glance at the man beside her. Kevin was frowning, his honey-colored brows drawn together as he maneuvered the horses. Somehow she didn't think the driving was taxing enough to take that amount of attention. He was obviously as deep in thought as she had been, and the thoughts did not seem pleasant. What if he had already decided that they did not suit?

She should have been relieved, she told herself sternly. She could go back to her everyday existence. She could forget about Almack's. She would not have to endure any more of these awkward social outings. She would never have to see him again.

The feelings in her throat worsened, as panic seized her. She forced it down and straightened in her seat with determination. She had been wishing for months, for perhaps her whole life, for an opportunity to make her mark on a man like Kevin Whattling. She was not about to let her chance slip away so easily.

"Mr. Whattling," she said. He shook himself out of his reverie and turned to face her. "I find I am in agreement with you. Driving with you has been, if not delightful, certainly an educational experience."

He chuckled. "I would thank you, Miss Welch, but I'm not sure that was a compliment."

"Ah, but you must remember, sir, that I am a bluestocking. To be educational is the highest compliment."

He acknowledged her sally with a nod of his head. "Then I thank you for the honor."

She returned his smile shyly, then realized as the silence stretched that she would have to say something if she wanted to continue the conversation, perhaps even his courting. She swallowed, and suddenly inspiration hit. She was the bluestocking after all. Perhaps it was time she started acting like it.

"I find I would like additional education," she told Kevin, "if you would be so kind."

Kevin looked puzzled. "About what?"

"The life of a Corinthian." When he looked stunned, she hurried on. "As I understand it, you Corinthians make a study out of sporting events much in the same the way we bluestockings make a study of scientific and artistic pursuits. I should like to compare our study habits. Perhaps you would be so kind as to join me for tea tomorrow?"

His look of surprise melted into his infectious grin. "If you wanted my company, Madam, you had merely to ask. You needn't subject yourself to a boring lesson in sports."

"Oh, I'm sure anything you'd have to say about it would hardly be boring," Eugennia began, then stopped, blushing furiously as she realized how sycophantic she must have sounded.

Kevin merely chuckled. "Very well, then, tea tomorrow and the life of a Corinthian."

Eugennia decided to say nothing further that might change his mind.

Seven

By the time Kevin arrived for a late afternoon tea the next day, Eugennia had herself sufficiently in hand to pour it. It had only taken her the rest of the evening to decide to wear her violet lustring with the white lace collar, and this with considerable help and advice from Miss Tindale.

"I simply do not understand why you are encouraging this fellow," her companion sniffed after Eugennia had had her search through the wardrobe for the third time. "Isn't he just another fortune hunter?"

Eugennia paused in her vain attempt to find the matching violet glove somewhere in the back of one of her dresser drawers. "To tell you the truth, Martha, I did think he was only that. But there is something about him. Remember what I was telling you the other day about my handsome prince?"

Martha narrowed her eyes to two gray slits surrounded by wrinkles. "Yes, and don't start on that again. I didn't understand it then—I doubt I will now."

"It really isn't all that difficult to understand," Eugennia told her, pulling her to sit beside her on the bed. "Who is the most handsome, charming man you've ever met?"

Martha blinked. "I . . . I suppose I've never thought about it before. There really isn't much chance of meeting such a paragon in my post." She noticed Eugennia regarding her and blushed. "No offense meant, of course."

"None taken," Eugennia assured her, watching her companion sadly. Could Martha really have given up on all dreams of love? She almost shuddered as she realized that in a few more years, she would be in exactly the same situation. She squared her shoulders. "I know. Remember when you read that novel last year and you thought the hero was the most elegant gentleman you had ever heard tell of?"

Martha's gray eyes shone. "Oh, yes," she breathed, clasping hands to her nearly flat bosom. "Now, there was a man."

"What would you do if he walked into your parlor and asked you to marry him?"

Martha stared at her, frozen. "But he can't—he's just a story."

Eugennia sighed and tried again. "But what if he was real, Martha? What if he wanted to marry you?"

"I wouldn't keep him waiting for an answer," Martha snapped. "You can be very sure of that."

Jenny laughed wryly, rising. "And here I am doing just that." She glanced around at the mess they had made of her meager wardrobe. "Yet I feel compelled to make a good impression on him. Wouldn't it be wonderful, Martha, if he could come to see me as his equal, his partner? Then I think I could accept his offer."

"He is very pleasant to look upon," Miss Tindale offered, watching her from the safety of the bed. "But I cannot trust a man who admits he is in debt."

Jenny shook her head. "Would you rather he hid the fact? I think he should be commended for being honest about it."

"Yes, but how did he get in such difficulties to begin

with?" Miss Tindale countered, wrinkling her long nose with distaste. "Was he a gambler? Did he throw it away on wicked women?"

"Both?" Jenny guessed, and Martha gasped. "Oh, really, Martha, even you cannot be so innocent as to believe a man as attractive and charismatic as Mr. Whattling lived as a monk. I daresay any number of young ladies have tried to attract his attention." The two debutantes from the park came readily to mind. "Besides, does it matter how he lost the money?"

Miss Tindale raised a wispy eyebrow. "Of course it matters! If his solicitor lost it on the Exchange with this business over Napoleon, that is one thing. But if Mr. Whattling was so precipitous as to gamble it away, that is something else entirely. In the first case, he is merely a poor judge of character. In the second, he *has* a poor character. If I were going to let him court me, I think I would want to know which it was."

"Perhaps you're right," Jenny mused, staring off into the middle distance. It was only logical, after all. She supposed she was being a bit odd again, but she often thought that marriage was like a partnership. Certainly she would have her solicitor Mr. Carstairs investigate any business partner she might want to take on. This would be no different.

"Ring for Mavis to come help us with these clothes, Martha," she declared, dusting off her hands. "Then you can help me pen a note to Mr. Carstairs to see to the matter. More information is always useful when trying to make a decision, I find."

After what she felt was a dismal showing during the drive the day before, Eugennia was determined that tea would be much more successful. She had some social skills, after all; she had only to portray them in the proper light. Accordingly, by the time Kevin Whattling arrived, she had set the stage to her satisfaction. Fiching in his polished black was at his station in the front hall, and Miss Tindale in her best navy bombazine was sitting properly as chaperone beside the tea cart in the sitting room. Eugennia had her silver tea service and bone china cups and saucers waiting at her side along with a tempting assortment of jellies, pastries, and tea cakes. Outwardly, she was sure she looked calm and composed, the very epitome of ladylike restraint. Inwardly she found herself in turmoil, although again the reason for it eluded her. She wondered if she could keep her hand from shaking while she poured.

Kevin arrived precisely at three. He hadn't had to borrow anything to make a good showing in his navy morning coat and trousers. After the way she had encouraged him to call the day before, he wasn't entirely sure what to expect. Part of him had hoped for a few moments alone in which to advance his suit, but he didn't let his disappointment show when he saw that the companion he had succeeded in avoiding the day before was now firmly installed at Miss Welch's right hand.

And she was a dragon.

It took only one glance at the narrowed eyes and pursed lips to determine that Miss Welch's companion had taken him in dislike. He had definitely blundered by not considering her sooner. In his experience, young ladies either cherished their companions as friends, relying on them for advice, or they ignored and avoided them whenever possible. Looking at the iron-haired woman sitting beside Eugennia, her thin frame as straight as a billiard cue, he somehow thought she was one who wasn't used to being ignored.

"Good afternoon, Mr. Whattling," Eugennia intoned as

he crossed the room to bow over her hand. "I don't believe you've met my companion, Miss Martha Tindale."

The dragon affixed him with a glare that could only be called icy. "Mr. Whattling," she sniffed.

Kevin bowed over her hand, feeling the frail bones beneath. The woman was older than she looked, which, Lord knew, was old enough. "Miss Tindale. I regret you couldn't join us yesterday for our drive."

"I'm sure you do," Miss Tindale replied, and they both knew she was being sarcastic.

"Please sit down, Mr. Whattling," Eugennia put in, frowning at Martha behind his back as he settled himself across from her. "It was good of you to come. Martha and I could hardly wait for our discussion."

Martha said nothing, but snorted derisively.

"A pleasure, as always," Kevin insisted. Charm was lost on Miss Tindale. Perhaps ignoring her was a better strategy after all. He steadfastly kept his eyes on Eugennia's ivory complexion and told himself sternly not to look at the dragon beside her. It didn't help that Miss Tindale had a long nose with a hook on the end and a rather large mole beside her right eye. When she squinted at him, as she was doing now, the hair in the center of the mole stood at attention. He smiled politely at Eugennia.

"Would you care for tea?" Eugennia asked, reaching for the silver pot. She was delighted to find her hand moved gracefully. Perhaps she could carry this off after all.

"Please," Kevin replied.

Miss Tindale sniffed again, and he swore the hook of her nose bounced against her thin lips. He wondered whether there would be room for the teacup.

"Milk or lemon?" Eugennia asked.

"Neither, thank you." He nodded his thanks as Eugennia handed him the china cup. She poured for Miss Tindale, who somehow managed to sip without dipping her nose in the stuff. Kevin looked hurriedly down at the cup.

"A lovely pattern," he managed. "English?"

"French," Eugennia replied. "It was my mother's."

"She obviously had the same excellent taste as her daughter," Kevin put in.

Suddenly, Eugennia wanted nothing more than to laugh. He was obviously trying so very hard to be charming, and she was just as obvious in her attempts to play the proper hostess. In attempting to capture his attentions, she was destroying the very spontaneity that had attracted her to him in the first place. She put up her chin, willing her wayward emotions to still. He had come courting her. She was still the one who decided whether he succeeded.

"I believe you would compliment this china," she told him, quirking a determined smile, "even if it was a hideous purple with gold cherubs about the rim."

"Eugennia!" Miss Tindale exclaimed.

"Oh, hush, Martha." She could see the answering smile in Kevin's eyes, and her remaining doubts vanished. "Mr. Whattling and I understand each other. He is courting me, so he has to utter rubbish. I, on the other hand, am in the fortunate position of being able to be as rude as I choose."

"Not that you'd ever be rude, of course," Kevin corrected her. "On the other hand, if you insist on baiting me, I could threaten to rhapsodize about your nose again."

"Your nose?" Martha blinked.

Eugennia giggled, relaxing against the chair and starting to enjoy herself. "No, please, not my nose. And not the weather, your friend's horses, or the interesting way in which you've tied your cravat. You promised to enlighten me about the ways of a Corinthian, sir. Have you forgotten?"

"No," Kevin sighed, setting his cup down on the cart. "But I was hoping you had. Do you truly wish me to go into what makes a Corinthian, Madam? Surely there are better things about which to converse."

"There certainly are," Miss Tindale muttered. Kevin ignored her.

"Nonsense," Eugennia told them both. "I explained to you yesterday that being educational was the highest compliment a bluestocking could give. So, please, Mr. Whattling, educate me."

She was playing with him—he could feel it. He ought to resent it, but some part of him relished the challenge. He wasn't such a beggar that he'd forgotten how to play the game. "Very well," he bowed. "The life of a Corinthian then. As you probably know, we are a breed enthralled with sporting pursuits."

"Such as?" Eugennia probed.

"Horse racing, carriage racing, yacht racing, boxing, card playing, dice." He rattled off every activity he could think of. "Cock fighting, dog fighting, bear baiting, wagering of any kind, dallying with the ladies."

"Good heavens," Miss Tindale exclaimed, taking a fortifying sip of tea.

"And do you excel in all of them?" Eugennia asked fascinated.

"Are you speaking of me personally," he teased, "or the breed in general, Miss Welch?"

Nothing would have given her more satisfaction than to hear about his own personal strengths, but she couldn't very well tell him that. "The Corinthian in general, sir, of course."

"Ah. Well, we do try to excel in all the manly arts, although some, I would say, do better than others."

"And I suppose you do them all disgustingly well," Martha grumbled.

He decided the safest thing was to take it as a compliment, even if her sarcasm was still evident. "Thank you, Miss Tindale. You are too kind."

"And which are your favorite pastimes?" Eugennia asked innocently while Martha glared.

Kevin grinned at her. "I'll let you guess."

Miss Tindale set her teacup down with a proprietary thump. "Horse racing," she wheezed.

He kept Eugennia's gaze. "That's one of them."

She knew what he wanted her to say. He wanted her to blurt out that he was a famous lady's man. She could feel a blush rising to her cheek, but she refused to look away. "Boxing," she put in defiantly.

His smile deepened. "Yes, of course. Boxing. How very perceptive, Miss Welch."

Miss Tindale shuddered, reaching for her teacup again. "Nasty sport. Striking each other until someone is unconscious. I never understood how anyone could watch it."

"It isn't a sport for the ladies," Kevin agreed, taking his own sip of tea.

"Do you fight often?" Eugennia asked, relieved to have gotten him onto a safer subject.

"Not anymore," he replied. "Nor do I do many of the other activities we discussed. I suppose you could say I have retired."

Miss Tindale's hair was standing at attention again as she frowned. "And why would you want to do that, if you were as good as you implied?"

"Let us say that I find other pursuits more urgent at the moment," he replied, but she saw a shadow cross his eyes. "And since you felt free to be rude earlier, Miss Welch, might I mention that I am particularly fond of raspberry jellies?"

She immediately helped him to some off the cart and listened as he skillfully maneuvered the conversation onto other subjects. His fingers touched hers for a second as she handed him the plate, and she felt a tingle run up her arm. He grinned at her as if he knew exactly how she felt. She looked away with a blush.

He was really the most amazing man, she reflected as he and Martha discussed the best poultices for bruised extremities. If he did half of those activities he'd named half as well as he implied, he had been every bit as much of a scholar as she was. Still, for all the conversation, she had gleaned few additional facts about the man. In fact, he was marvelously skilled in conversing on a variety of topics while imparting little hint as to his own feelings on the matter. He may have claimed boxing as his favorite pastime, but she suspected otherwise. Mr. Kevin Whattling was born to charm. The question was, just how far was she willing to let his charm take him?

Eight

Nigel and Giles met at White's that night as they usually did, but they went out of their way to slip unseen into high-backed chairs at one of the farthest tables. They were so circumspect, in fact, that only one other gentleman noticed them, and he was so curious that he found his way silently to the chair nearest theirs to observe.

"I understand from my man that he saw her again today," Giles reported, wiggling to squeeze his bulk more effectively into the armchair.

"Good thing you thought to set your footman after them," Nigel commented. "Rather embarrassing being caught like that in the park the other day. I felt like some demmed gossiping fishwife."

"Well, we had to do something," Giles protested. "We had to be sure that Kevin would succeed. We owe him that as his friends."

"You'll get no argument from me," Nigel grumbled. "If we'd done our duty earlier, Robbie might still be alive."

Giles paled. "Yes, well, as you say. But getting back to the matter at hand, if Kevin saw her today, that's three days in a row. Don't you think that's a good sign?"

"Could be," Nigel allowed, signaling to a passing attendant to bring them port. "Unfortunately, Kevin does not have the luxury of tarrying. I took the liberty of checking about, and I heard from Tallyrand that Kevin hasn't paid the rent on his flat, among a few other bills. The creditors he couldn't pay are beginning to make noises about serving notice. If he's determined to marry that woman, he'd better be quick about it."

Giles shivered. "Women are so unpredictable. She could keep him dangling for months."

"We don't have months!" Nigel almost shouted, smacking his fist on the tabletop. "I tried to tell him he didn't have time for this foolishness. Besides, he never plans ahead. I admire a man of action, but Kevin thinks entirely too much in the moment, if he thinks at all!"

Giles chewed his lower lip thoughtfully. "Still, we cannot desert him. There must be something we can do. I don't suppose we could help things along?"

"What do you mean?" Nigel demanded with his milk-curdling frown.

"I'm not sure," Giles replied. "It's just an idea, really. But don't women generally expect little gifts and flowers? Tokens of appreciation? Kevin can scarcely provide her with that. But we could. Nothing out of taste, of course."

"Of course," Nigel nodded, looking off into the distance. "Nothing personal or expensive. A real lady wouldn't accept them. But flowers, you said. We might be able to manage flowers."

"And chocolates?" Giles brightened.

Nigel nodded again, more firmly this time. "Certainly. Capital idea, Giles. Make the arrangements in the morning and have them send the bill to my establishment. And of course you will sign Kevin's name to everything."

"I'm not totally lack-witted," Giles told him with annoyance. "You can be sure that Kevin will be given all the credit."

And well he should be, George Safton thought, rising from

the chair behind theirs and strolling away before they could catch sight of him. Trust Kevin to find an easy way out of this mess. A rich spinster, no less. He had thought that was Eugennia Welch driving with Kevin the other day in Hyde Park. From the sound of it, it was an all-out assault—three visits in as many days. No woman of his acquaintance could have withstood Kevin's considerable charms. Certainly an old biddy like Eugennia Welch would be in transports. She was probably already picking the wedding dress.

But marriage was the last thing George wanted for Kevin. Of course, some men would have been able to put Miss Welch's fortune to good use. And marriage was often a convenient place from which to conduct any number of lively affairs. But if George knew Kevin, he'd probably be true to the hag until death did them part. And he would probably stay by her side each night reading God-knew-what ponderous tome designed to edify her mind and lure Kevin to sleep in minutes. That would keep him and her fortune away from the gambling tables, the boxing, and any other sport George might care to dream up. It was a deuced nuisance.

Besides, George wasn't sure he wanted to give up his favorite plaything just yet. The loss of Robert Greene was still too fresh. Nasty business that. He had been implicated, and that had put a decided dent in his activities. People who had cast a blind eye on his way of living in the past now asked entirely too many questions. Where he was once welcomed to White's and any other establishment he might choose to frequent, now more often he was shunned.

He had no doubt part of the problem was Kevin's attempt to get the magistrates interested in the boxing matches he arranged on occasion. That attempt had failed, but fewer gentlemen stood ready to participate, with their fists or with their wallets, which was more important to him. Kevin's continued companionship would surely help improve his standing. Without that veneer of respectability, he might not be able to gain entrance to all the places he needed to be to find appropriate people upon whom to work his wiles. No, Kevin Whattling was crucial to George's plans, and George wasn't about to let him slip into peaceful matrimony so easily.

So, what to do? He strolled toward a group playing cards, and the men hurriedly finished their game and left. Taking one of the vacated chairs, he thumbed idly through the deck of abandoned cards, just as his mind thumbed through plans. Whattling had resisted any overt efforts at reconciliation, so there seemed no point trying that again. The better approach seemed to be foiling his plans with the heiress. George smiled, and seeing his smile, another two men hurriedly quit the room. If Miss Welch was interested in being courted, George had no difficulty in obliging her. He didn't think he need go so far as to marry her, of course, but if she suddenly became damaged goods and Kevin Whattling lost interest in the woman in the process, that was all to the benefit.

The remaining gentlemen in the room heaved a collective sigh of relief as George "The Snake" Safton strolled out of the door for the evening, in search of bigger prey.

Eugennia strolled along Curzon Street in her dove-colored pelisse, with Miss Tindale in black at her side and Stevens their footman behind her. Her usual constitutional wasn't nearly as refreshing today as she had hoped. She didn't have to analyze much to determine why. Kevin Whattling hadn't mentioned yesterday when he intended to call again. As he had done so at every other visit, she was afraid that the omission could only mean he had lost interest in calling. She tried to tell herself it was all to the good, but she was feeling terribly dejected by the whole affair.

It was impossible not to feel as if she were somehow lacking. While her fortune had been enough to get him to call in the first place, obviously it could only have been her presence that had stopped him from calling. She couldn't help wondering what about her had offended him. Had she been too forward, not forward enough? Had her conversation repulsed him as too pedantic, or too frivolous? Or worse, had she been unable to arouse any return of feeling? He'd claimed he wanted to feel some sort of affection for the woman he was being forced to marry. Most likely the only thing he felt for her was pity: pity for the rich spinster who didn't know how to go about in society. She shivered in her pelisse, pulled her silk shawl more closely about her, and increased her stride.

"Eugennia, please, slow down!" Martha moaned, struggling to keep up. "Is there somewhere we must be? Are we late for some appointment?"

"No, Martha," she sighed, forcing her steps to slow. "We aren't late for anything. We have no appointments. No one will care if we arrive anywhere, at any time."

"What do you mean? Of course someone would care. What if we were late for Miss St. John's discussion group?" Martha caught up to her and peered at her sideways. "Are you out of countenance again? It's this Kevin Whattling fellow, isn't it?"

Despite herself, Eugennia felt her stride lengthening again. She shoved her gloved hands deeper in the fur muff in determination. "I do not wish to speak about him, if you please," she tossed back over her shoulder.

"But Eugennia!" Martha all but wailed.

Eugennia ignored her. She had had enough. It was ridiculous to think she could completely change her life by meeting the right gentleman. Mr. Whattling could have been that gentleman, and all he'd done was turn her world topsy turvy. Why, he even had her doubting her own intelligence! It was not to be borne. She put all her energy into walking, her sturdy half boots stalking along, and she was soon several lengths ahead of Martha and her footman. Belatedly, she realized she was being terribly rude. It was hardly poor Martha's fault. She decided to go only as far as the corner of Curzon and Park Lane and wait. However, she hadn't even reached the corner when a young boy in ragged trousers leapt out in front of her, ramming into her. She gasped, but as she tried to right herself, he snatched her muff and tore it from her grasp.

"What are you doing?" she demanded.

The boy turned a dirty face to hers, baring his teeth and growling like some kind of animal. Even as she shrunk back in horror, he reached for the ivory broach on the shoulder of her pelisse.

"Stop that!" a strong masculine voice ordered, and the boy's eyes widened in fear. He dropped Eugennia's muff and dashed off up the street, almost immediately hidden from view among the passersby on Park Lane. Eugennia swayed, and two strong arms caught her. "Careful now. Everything will be all right."

"Jenny!" Martha cried, hurrying up, panting, with Stevens just ahead of her. "Are you hurt! What did that awful brat do to you?"

"I'm all right, Martha," Eugennia managed, not at all sure of the truth of that statement. It had all happened so quickly that she wasn't sure what she felt. Her rescuer set her on her feet and bent to retrieve her muff. She turned to find herself regarding a vaguely familiar handsome gentleman with raven hair and eyes just as dark. He wasn't nearly as handsome as Kevin Whattling, of course, but his chin was more square, his chest in the gray coat and white waistcoat broader, and his smile even more charming.

"Please excuse my interference," he was murmuring, bowing to her and Martha in turn. "I couldn't sit idly by and watch a woman be accosted."

"Certainly not," Martha sniffed. "We are forever in your debt, sir, er . . ."

"Safton," he bowed again. "George Safton."

"Miss Eugennia Welch," Jenny managed, still a little shaken. "And my companion, Miss Martha Tindale."

"Ladies, a pleasure," he nodded, handing Eugennia her muff. "And may I say that it is a sad day for London when two such lovely young ladies cannot walk a city street unmolested."

Martha beamed at him.

Eugennia managed a smile. His attempt to charm was even more obvious than Kevin's had been. In fact, Mr. Safton made it seem even easier.

"Thank you, Mr. Safton, for your assistance," she told him. "We should not take up any more of your time. Martha?"

"Please, Miss Welch," he swiftly countered, stepping to block her way. "I would not count myself a gentleman if I did not see you safely home. May I not walk at least a little way with you, just to make sure you're all right?"

It seemed a bit encroaching, but Martha was preening and truth be told, Jenny wasn't averse to having someone else in their party. She couldn't imagine what the boy had been thinking to attack her like that, and it made her wonder what else might suddenly jump out on her way home. "Very well, then, Mr. Safton. This way."

He offered her his arm, and they strolled back down Curzon, deeper into Mayfair. The neat town houses marched along beside them, each one brick and stone, looking so respectable that she found it difficult to believe she had been attacked so close to their solid front doors.

"The weather is certainly lovely for this time of year," Mr. Safton remarked.

"How very astute of you to notice, Mr. Safton," Martha replied in admiration. Eugennia hid a smile.

"It is difficult not to notice, dear lady, with the sunshine brightening the walk and showing us all the lovely works of nature." He included her and Martha in the statement, just as Kevin would have done, but somehow the sentiment did not ring true. She stole a look at him out of the corner of her eye, but he was glancing at their surroundings. She looked away, only to continue her walk with the uncanny feeling that it was she who was being watched.

George, on the other hand, was feeling quite pleased with himself. Using the street urchin had been a stroke of genius, if he did say so himself. He couldn't imagine why Kevin hadn't already convinced her to elope to Gretna Green with him; she was obviously an innocent, and a gullible one at that. And she wasn't nearly the ape leader he had thought. The spring sunlight brought out gold highlights in the ash blond curls escaping from her straw bonnet and when she peered at him with those large hazel eyes of hers, he could think of a number of ways to get her to marry him in far less time than Kevin was taking. Still, it was better to stick to his plan. His goal was to retrieve the wayward Kevin, not capture Miss Eugennia Welch.

"Miss Welch," he ventured after they had walked some way, "I believe we have a mutual friend. Do you know a Mr. Kevin Whattling by any chance?"

Eugennia tried not to bridle, but she saw a light spring up in the man's eyes and knew she must have betrayed herself. "Yes, I do. Is he a good friend of yours, Mr. Safton?"

"A very dear friend, at least, until recently."

She shouldn't rise to the bait, but she couldn't help herself. "Recently? What changed?"

He had her—he could feel it. Yet something warned him not to mention Robbie. If she had known Kevin was only recently out of mourning, she would most likely have brought it up at his probing. If he were the one to break it to her, he might inadvertently put Kevin in the role of martyr.

"I believe he may be having some kind of financial difficulty," he replied instead. "Nothing serious, one would hope, or I'm sure he'd have come to me for assistance. Of course, Kevin is an ingenious man, as I'm sure you know. If he can't find one way to raise the funds, I'm sure he'll find another."

"Perhaps he'll find a rich heiress to wed," Eugennia replied acidly.

Martha gasped and turned the move into a coughing fit. Stevens obligingly thumped her on the back until she waved him off.

Safton eyed Eugennia. That tone could only mean she knew. Drat Kevin for being painfully honest. He tried another tact. "Oh, certainly not. Kevin Whattling would never stoop so low as to marry a woman for her money. He isn't the type to offer praise where none is warranted."

She was blushing, and he knew he had scored. Thinking of what Giles and Nigel had planned, he warmed to his theme. "No. Kevin is an honest fellow, at least he has been with any woman I've seen him with, and I've seen him with quite a few. He doesn't send flowers or chocolates or hang about in the lady's pocket day after day, as if he did not trust her to think without him. He's that sort of fellow."

"Yes," Eugennia murmured, angry at the tears that seemed to be welling behind her eyes, "I somehow thought he was."

Safton beamed at her. "Well, then, we are in agreement. Kevin Whattling is a jolly good fellow. Perhaps we can all go for a drive some time."

She stopped and turned to him. "I don't know when I'll next be seeing Mr. Whattling. If you see him before I do, Mr. Safton, will you let him know that I'm not expecting him. It's a rather odd message, I know, but I think he'll understand."

George frowned convincingly. "Are you sure, Madam? You almost sound as if you were dismissing him."

She managed a laugh, but it sounded brittle even to her own ears. "Oh, la, sir, one cannot dismiss what one never had."

"Miss Welch? I hope I haven't said something to upset you."

"Not at all, Mr. Safton. You have eased my mind—you have no idea. We are almost home now, and I feel quite recovered. I cannot in good conscience detain you any longer."

He bowed over her hand. She was sending him packing, but he had done what he had set out to accomplish that day. "Of course. Your servant, Madam. And yours as well, Miss Tindale."

Martha simpered.

He started to turn away, but he caught the glint of unshed tears in her eyes and for some reason the day didn't seem quite so successful. Good God, was one walk in the company of a bluestocking enough to give him a case of morals? He had better act to ensure his progress before it got any worse. "I hope you won't mind," he put in as she started to pass him, "if I call tomorrow, just to see that you are indeed unharmed from today's escapade?"

She ought to depress any notions he might have right now, but the fact that a handsome fellow might actually prefer her company was balm to her wounds. What harm could it do? "That is very kind of you, Mr. Safton. Say three?"

"Three it is. Until then, ladies." He strolled back the way they had come, and she thought she heard him begin to whistle.

"Well, at least someone's happy today," she remarked to Martha as she trudged wearily toward home.

Nine

Kevin knew that the best way to ensure his suit was progressing was to lavish his attention on Eugennia. Calling daily was a bit scandalous, but he didn't have much time and he had made his intentions abundantly clear. He wasn't sure what had possessed him not to make an appointment before he left the day before. She didn't seem the type to enjoy impromptu associations. When he woke around noon that next day, he had every intention of dressing leisurely and strolling over to Mayfair to dance attendance on the lady.

One swipe of his comb through his hair changed all that.

There was a gray hair caught in the comb.

He stared at it for some minutes, bemused. Somehow he hadn't expected one until after his thirtieth birthday, which was still several years away. Gray hairs, everyone knew, were caused by the excessive worrying that came with advancing age. Up until Robbie had become obsessed with gambling, Kevin hadn't had a care in the world. If the events surrounding his brother's death hadn't been able to raise a gray hair on his head, what on earth was he doing now that would do so?

The answer was, of course, that he was courting Eugennia.

Now that was a leveler. What was it about courting that made him turn gray? He knew any number of his fellow Corinthians who claimed that becoming leg-shackled, as they termed matrimony, was the end of a fellow's life. He had never seen it as such. Marriage to him had always seemed like the beginning of some new venture—two people agreeing to live for each other, instead of themselves. He smiled, thinking of Nigel and Giles' stunned reactions if he had ever admitted to such heretical beliefs.

So if it wasn't the courting, it could only be the woman he had chosen to court. That, unfortunately, made even less sense. The lady was every bit as delightful as he had thought she would be, if in a different way. Why should the fact that she was witty and adorably innocent make him worry enough to get a gray hair? He ought to rejoice in the fact that she was such a taking little thing. Most of their conversations made him laugh and the others made him think, a pleasant change from his usual conversations with his own set. He had hoped the touch of his hand would make her blush, but was surprised to find that the touch of her hand made his heart race as if he were a green schoolboy, and not an experienced lover. He had hoped to eventually grow fond of her, but twice now he had caught himself wondering what it would be like to kiss her, more, to hold her womanly curves against his chest through the night. He tried in vain to convince himself he was a lucky fellow—she was warm, rich, and delectable. Why should that bother him in the least?

Perhaps it was his own behavior that was wanting. He couldn't say he hadn't been honest. He had told her from the beginning he was looking to wed a wealthy woman. And he had told her he wanted to care about the woman. Neither of those facts had changed. She had seemed amenable to the idea, even if she wasn't entirely sure of its truth as yet. He knew his nearness affected her, but he hadn't taken advantage of that fact to compromise her with forbidden touches or secret kisses (although he couldn't say he hadn't contemplated how enjoyable that might be). Everything was completely aboveboard.

He tried to think of anything he had said that he hadn't meant. He had never complimented her when she did not deserve it. He had never praised anything that wasn't worthy of praise. He never claimed to like something that he despised. He had been completely honest.

So, what was bothering him?

He chased the questions for much of the afternoon, then realized that he had fretted away any time he might have spent with Eugennia. He would have liked to talk things over with Nigel or Giles, but as the only mirror he had left was barely big enough to shave by, let alone see if there were any more telltale gray hairs, he was loath to try to find them. Besides, what was he to say to them?

Reluctantly, he let the questions lie that night, but by morning he was no closer to answers. However, finding a notice from his landlord that his rent was now three weeks overdue did nothing to lighten his mood. Through a stern conversation, he managed to convince himself that he ought to feel rather annoyed at these ruminations. He had set himself upon this path for a reason. The reason had not changed. The path was still a logical one. With determination, he dressed in a bottle green coat with fawn trousers and tan waistcoat and strolled over to Eugennia Welch's town house to continue what he had set out to do.

He knew she wasn't expecting him, but he wasn't expecting the scene that greeted him. A florist's lorry stood at the curb, horses standing and muttering. The front door of the town house was swinging open with no one in attendance. He clapped the brass knocker anyway, but no one answered his summons. Concerned, he poked his head into the entry, but found it as empty as the staircase beyond.

"Fiching?" he called, echo rising with his concern. "Miss Welch? Miss Tindale? Is anyone home?"

"Mr. Whattling!" Miss Tindale responded, appearing from a doorway to the left. Her arms were so full of white lilies that all he could see was the top of her iron gray head and the bottom of her black skirts. She had never looked better. "Somehow I knew you would show up to take credit! Now I suppose we will have to thank you personally."

"Thank me, Madam?" He frowned. But she hurried past him across the entry toward the sitting room. Fiching appeared in her wake, balancing a rather large silver urn of bright gardenias in one arm and a Chinese vase full of pink carnations in the other.

"Oh, Mr. Whattling, sir. I'm sorry to say our footmen are all busy, but I'll be with you in just a moment." He teetered up the stairs and disappeared overhead. A young man in an apprentice's apron backed out of the same room.

"That's the lot, then, Miss Welch. Will you be needing anything else?"

"Only a dozen more vases," Eugennia replied, following him out into the hall, her arms full of red roses that clashed with the violet silk of her morning dress. "But I think we have that many about somewhere. Thank you for your help."

"You're very welcome, ma'am." He tipped his cap and turned to go, nearly colliding with the bemused Kevin. "Beggin' yer pardon, gov'nor."

Kevin nodded as he skittered past. Eugennia blushed as

red as her roses. Kevin stepped forward, offering her his best smile. "Lovely roses, Miss Welch."

"All the flowers are lovely, Mr. Whattling," she replied. "Lovely, but not wanted in the least."

Before he could respond to her curious remark, Fiching clattered back down the stairs. "Let me take those, Miss Jenny."

Jenny, Kevin thought with a smile as she handed them hurriedly over. It suited her far more than Eugennia. When she gave him permission to call her by her first name, that's the name he'd use.

"You really shouldn't have, Mr. Whattling," she told him as Fiching dashed off to the nether regions of the house. "I'm fond of flowers, but this is a bit much."

"I'm rather fond of flowers myself," Kevin replied. "But I assure you, I didn't send you roses."

She made a face. "And will you tell me that you didn't send the three dozen lilies, four dozen carnations, or six dozen gardenias?"

Kevin raised an eyebrow. "Someone sent you one hundred and fifty-six flowers?"

"One hundred and eighty, if one is to count the two dozen roses," Eugennia corrected him. "There is no need to dissemble, sir. Your card came with each batch."

"Did it?" he murmured, frowning. He could think of only two people who knew of his plans with Jenny, but even they would not go so far as to order one hundred and eighty flowers. There had to be some mistake.

"Are you sure it was my card?" he asked. "Surely your other suitors send flowers. Perhaps there was a mistake at the florist's."

She paled and her jaw tightened. "I have no other suitors, Mr. Whattling, as if you didn't know. Are you intent on making a fool of me?"

He recoiled before her vehemence. "I assure you, Miss Welch, nothing could be farther from my mind. Much as I'd love to shower you with flowers, and any number of other gifts if you'd let me, I haven't the blunt. Can you imagine what roses must cost at the beginning of March?"

She frowned. "You have a point." She refused to let him see how much his innocence meant to her. "But if you did not send them, who did?"

"I may have an idea. May I ask, did you look at the cards closely?"

She shrugged. "Enough to see that it was your signature."

He smiled. "My signature, eh? And did all the handwriting look the same?"

Eugennia started, then gazed at him more closely. The grin was entirely too confident; he had obviously learned something from their conversation. "I never looked."

"Then pray do so. For that matter, show the cards to me as well. I'd love to see how good a forger our mysterious benefactor is."

She led him into the library, mind whirling. When the delivery wagons had begun arriving that morning, her heart had sunk even farther, if that was possible. Mr. Safton had been right—Kevin thought so little of her that he thought he could flatter his way into her life with a few roses and some excellent chocolate. But lilies had followed roses, carnations had followed lilies, and gardenias had followed carnations until every room in her town house but the library boasted at least one vase. The perfume was overpowering and a little contradictory, and even now the footmen and maids were scurrying about opening windows. She scolded herself for not pausing to analyze the situation. Of course he couldn't have afforded so many flowers, if his debts were as great as he claimed. The question was, why would anyone else possibly want to send flowers for him?

She went to sit at her father's leather padded desk beside the large windows and motioned Kevin to the armchair flanking it.

"May I have a quill and paper?" Kevin asked as he was seated.

She pulled them and the ink from the drawer in the desk and pushed them across the surface toward him. Leaning forward, he dipped the quill in the ink and scrawled his name across the page. Blotting the work, he pushed it back to her.

"And now the cards?"

She drew the cards from a pocket of her gown and slid them toward him. Kevin thumbed through them thoughtfully.

"Well, we seem to have two friends, at the very least," he mused. "There, see for yourself."

She took the cards and laid them alongside his signature on the paper. The signature on the first card was cramped and tiny, as if the person wasn't sure he was allowed to sign that name and didn't exactly want to call attention to it. The signature on the second card was bold and black, the ink leaking through in places, the arrogant scrawl of a man who didn't care what others thought of him. The signature on the paper was elegant and firm, without affectation. They had clearly been made by three different people.

"But who would want to send flowers and gifts for you, Mr. Whattling?" she frowned.

Kevin sat back, relieved at her assessment. "I'm not sure. You said gifts. May I ask what?"

"Chocolate. Rather good chocolate. Actually, rather sinfully good chocolate. I didn't know they made it that well in London."

Kevin nodded. "Giles. My friend Giles Sloane has a secret stash from France. He gets it regularly. I don't ask questions."

"I wouldn't," Eugennia agreed. "And the other?"

Kevin stretched. "I don't recognize the handwriting, but I assume it is no doubt another friend. We were seen in Hyde Park together the other day by a great number of my acquaintances, and it is well know that if I were seriously courting a lady, I would have no funds to treat her as she would no doubt deserve, Miss Welch. I haven't done much courting, but I believe it is customary for the gentleman to send flowers and bring little gifts."

She looked away from him. "Perhaps customary, in some circumstances. I would prefer that you did not." This was her chance. She could stop all this nonsense with a single sentence, if she had the courage. Over the last day, she had come to realize that her emotions were entirely too volatile where Mr. Kevin Whattling was concerned. Her reactions were very unlike the bluestocking she prided herself in being. Time and again she had to remind herself to think rather than to simply react. Worse, she had been willing to compromise her own intelligence to gain his attention, behaving like some middle-aged woman who didn't realize she was no longer a dewy debutante. The mere thought sickened her. Much as she had wanted to have him court her, however much she had dreamed of him, she had to bring this business to an end before it affected her any more deeply. Suddenly her old life, however staid, seemed far less dangerous than being courted by Kevin Whattling.

"In fact, Mr. Whattling," she stated with determination, "I would prefer that you not call again."

Kevin sat straighter, color draining. He knew it had been a mistake to have spent a day musing; he should have consolidated his advantage. He should have known better than to give a bluestocking time to think. Now, thanks to Giles and Nigel's well-meaning interference, he was through. However fond he had become of Miss Welch, she obviously hadn't become as fond of him. "You're giving me the sack."

"You were never an employee. I therefore cannot sack you." He sat so still, lovely eyes unfocused, that she almost lost courage. "It has just been made apparent to me," she informed him, more to convince herself than anything else, "that we will not suit."

"I see," Kevin managed, when in truth he wasn't sure he saw anything but the fact that he had lost. The bitterness welling up in him spilled over into his words. "Well, if being away from you for one day and then having well-meaning friends fill your home with flowers so annoys you, I can well imagine we won't suit." He rose. "Thank you for your honesty, Madam. Another woman might have kept me dangling indefinitely. I admire your candor. Good day, Miss Welch." He bowed and walked out of the room while he still could.

Just like that, Eugennia thought, starting to shake. He hadn't even tried to dissuade her. No promises of undying devotion, no cries of dismay. He didn't even care enough to lie. She scolded herself for being ridiculous. He had been honest to the end, and she had sent him packing anyway. The princess had rejected the handsome prince, who had taken his white horse and nobly ridden off. Somehow she had thought stories weren't supposed to end that way.

Ten

George Safton arrived in the late afternoon to inquire about Eugennia's health. His navy coat and fawn trousers were calculated to remind her of Kevin Whattling's usual morning attire. Although he refrained from remarking on it, he noted the red and puffy eyes and trembling lip with satisfaction. Something was definitely wrong, which could only mean that things were working to his advantage. But he had never been one to rest on his achievements.

"I'm very glad to see that your misencounter the other day has had no ill effects," he replied when she assured him she was all right. "A lady cannot be too careful in these trying times."

"Don't I always say it," Miss Tindale agreed beside Eugennia on the sofa, patting down the skirts of her black bombazine.

Eugennia managed a wan smile. "I assure you, Mr. Safton, between Martha and Fiching, I'm in very good hands."

"It is a blessing to have true friends," Safton nodded, letting his smile include her companion and butler. Miss Tindale was beaming at him, so he had clearly won her over. The butler was scowling at him, but he didn't suppose that mattered much. "And speaking of friends, you haven't by any chance seen our mutual friend Mr. Whattling recently?"

He had the satisfaction of hearing Miss Tindale sniff derisively, while Eugennia paled until her skin clashed with the violet silk gown she was wearing.

"I do not expect to see Mr. Whattling again in the near future," she replied.

He sighed, keeping his triumph to himself. "Pity. I've been having a great deal of trouble catching up with him. He had mentioned wanting to catch Kean at Drury Lane with me. I went so far as to procure three tickets—for myself, Mr. Whattling, and his friend Mr. Sloane, but neither of them have sent word they will be able to attend. I do so hate attending the theater alone. One feels so out of place."

Miss Tindale sighed in understanding. Miss Welch was studying her hands folded in her lap.

"I don't suppose . . ." He looked as pathetic as he was able. "No, no, a great inconvenience, I'm sure."

"What?" Martha demanded. "Surely, Mr. Safton, you know that we would be happy to do you a service. Why, you saved Miss Jenny's life."

Jenny, he thought with disgust. *What an utterly plebeian name.* Still, if it would advance his cause, he ought to make use of it. "Not at all, Miss Tindale. I only sought to provide what minimal assistance I could. Your Miss Jenny should feel in no way beholden."

No, I shouldn't, Eugennia told herself firmly, sneaking a peak at the dark profile from under lowered lashes. She wasn't sure what it was about the man, but she didn't completely trust him. The smiles he was so eager to bestow never seemed to lighten the dark in his eyes. Still, he had been very kind the other day and quite thoughtful to check up on her well-being.

"If there's something you need, Mr. Safton," she told him, "I will do what I can to help."

"Would you do me the honor of joining me at the theater tomorrow evening?" he asked.

Martha clapped her hands. "What a splendid thought! May we, Eugennia?"

Eugennia looked from Martha's eager face to Safton's hopeful one. She had no desire to do anything but retire to her room and continue to cry, but that experience hadn't even been satisfying. She was quite partial to Edmund Kean's acting, and company other than Martha might be enjoyable. What harm could it do?

"Thank you, Mr. Safton," she nodded. "That would be a very nice diversion."

Giles and Nigel couldn't stand not knowing how well their handiwork had done. They invited Kevin to dinner at Nigel's apartments, where they were sure not to be disturbed by the odious George Safton. By that time, Kevin had managed to regain his composure. *It was all to the good,* he told himself, although he wasn't sure he'd be able to convince himself of that for a while. He consoled himself with the fact that the next heiress might not cause such havoc with his conscience.

But he couldn't let Giles off the hook so easily. Much as he admired his friend's generosity and willingness to help, he felt he needed to make a statement regarding the privacy of his actions. Thus as the dinner wore on, he refused to volunteer information, and he turned aside any subtle attempt to bring his courtship of Miss Welch into the conversation. Even though Nigel's dining room was spacious and decorated in cool colors, both his friends were soon adjusting their cravats and squirming in their walnut seats as if the quarters were a bit too cramped. By the time Nigel's liveried footmen were serving the third course, neither of them could stand to wait.

"But have you seen Miss Welch today?" Giles finally blurted out. Nigel glowered at him from the head of the long table, but he manfully refused to cringe. "That is, how is your courtship going?"

"When did you say Evalina Turnpeth was returning to town?" Kevin asked Nigel, taking a bite of his host's excellent beef.

Nigel stopped glowering long enough to blink. "June or July, I'm told. Didn't you hear Giles?"

"Most assuredly," Kevin smiled, nodding at his rotund friend across the damask-draped table. "I would never ignore you, Giles. I thought perhaps you'd take the hint. I need the name of another heiress."

Now it was Giles turn to frown. "Why?"

Nigel coughed. "Miss Welch turned you out, did she? I must say I gave her more credit than that."

"It was the flowers, wasn't it?" Giles groaned, paling and collapsing against the back of the Sheridan chair. "Oh, Kev, I'm so sorry! I was only trying to help!"

Kevin waved the issue aside with his spoon. "Don't concern yourself, Giles. We were fast approaching this junction in any event. Although, I must say, flowers from both of you was a bit too much."

Giles hung his head until his double chins were resting on the front of his white evening shirt. "It was only some roses. And I did put in some of my chocolate."

"Yes, well, that went over very nicely, as you might suppose." Kevin eyed his friend thoughtfully. "Am I to understand, then, that neither of you sent carnations, gardenias, or lilies?"

"Certainly not," Nigel sniffed. "Lilies are for the elderly, gardenias are insipid things, and carnations are highly unoriginal."

"Of course," Kevin allowed with a half smile, his mind busy. He could not think who else knew of his plans and would want to help. However, since it made little difference, he decided not to pursue it. She had turned him out, as Giles had guessed, and there wasn't much hope that that would change.

"Contradictory female," Nigel muttered. "If her tastes are so refined as to be upset by a few flowers, you're well rid of her."

"Hear, hear," Giles seconded. "Who will you try next, Kev?"

"Don't encourage him," Nigel scolded. "Kevin, this plan was ill-conceived from the first. Surely there must be something else you can do. What about Lord Hastings in the War Office? Hadn't he asked you to join him, in a somewhat unofficial capacity?"

"As a spy in France, you mean?" Kevin smiled. "Yes, several times. But the war is over. Napoleon is safely on Elba, and the Congress in Vienna is busily carving up his holdings. I don't imagine Hastings has much for me to do. Besides, I hear he is entirely too busy trying to get his son Leslie away from the gaming set before his great-aunt, Lady Martell, finds out."

"I say, I think you're a bit hard on Leslie Petersborough," Giles put in. "That Chas Prestwick fellow he hangs about with is nothing like George Safton."

Kevin regarded him silently. Nigel scowled. Giles sunk behind the silver epergne in the center of the table.

"Nevertheless, Kevin," Nigel continued, "you have to keep trying. There must be something you can turn your hand to to raise this money."

Kevin shook his head. "Not quickly enough, Nigel. And

despite what I said about Lord Hastings, chucking everything to leave for France feels too much like running away."

"And marrying some female for her money feels more manly?" Nigel demanded.

"Damnation!" Kevin swore, throwing down his napkin and rising. "I'm sick and tired of being lectured to. I got myself into this mess, and I will get myself out. And I'll thank the two of you to stay out of it!"

Giles started to protest, but Kevin didn't stop to hear whether it was an apology or agreement with Nigel. He stormed out of the room, sending one of the footman flying for his top hat and cloak. His foot was on the step when Giles caught up with him.

"Don't go like that!" he begged, jowls quivering. "We're your friends, Kev. Nigel means no harm."

"Then he should stay out of my affairs," Kevin growled, turning to leave. "You both ought to have more faith in me."

"Fanny Brighton turned down the duke," Giles replied.

Kevin stopped, looking back over his shoulder at him. "What?"

"Fanny Brighton, the gel Nigel says has buck teeth and laughs like a horse. I heard she turned down the duke because he didn't have enough dash. She's worth twenty thousand per annum."

Kevin stepped back and clapped him on the shoulder. "Thank you, Giles. I appreciate your confidence." He turned once more to go, and felt the tug of annoyance that Giles's faith hadn't lightened his steps.

"And Kevin," Giles called, "this time, I'll wait on the chocolate until you give me leave."

"You might as well give it to me now, old boy," Kevin laughed. "I have a feeling that this time, I'll need it."

* * *

As it turned out, not even Giles's excellent chocolate could have helped Kevin during his visit to the Brightons' the next afternoon. In fact, he quit the house so thankfully that he found himself walking entirely too fast toward his own apartments on St. James and forced himself to slow to his usual stroll. *Egads, what a creature!* He shuddered inside his navy morning coat just thinking about his close call. Whatever had possessed Giles to recommend her?

Miss Fanny Brighton did indeed have a set of prominent front teeth. Her laugh, he had decided, was much closer to the bray of a mule than the whinny of a horse. Either of those traits would have not been important to him, however, if she had been a pleasant person. But Miss Brighton was painfully aware of her position on the marriage mart, and she evaluated every gentleman who showed interest to see what a bargain she was buying.

From the first moment he had been ushered into the sitting room, he had felt as if he were on the block. The room, which was decorated after the Chinese style in vibrant shades of blue and red with satin draping nearly every surface, seemed hot and crowded, much more so than Jenny's sunny sitting room, even though the only people in it were Miss Brighton and her mother. Both of them were as overdressed as the room, their silk gowns sporting any number of laces and bows and ribbons until he wasn't sure what color the underlying fabric was. Unlike Miss Tindale, Mrs. Brighton could barely contain her eagerness at his call, small pudgy hands fluttering like two overweight butterflies at every sentence he uttered. However, he was quick to notice that those tiny dark eyes in a round face were much more calculating than her flighty manner indicated. They were every bit as calculating as the questions her daughter asked ever so innocently.

He was able to answer most of them straightforwardly

enough. After his experience with Eugennia, he was even more determined to behave as honestly as possible. However, as she quizzed him about his family, his education, and his connections, he began to have the perverse desire to say something outrageous. There was something about the proprietary smile that seemed to grow larger with each response he gave that made him long to wipe it off her face.

"I haven't seen you about much of late, Mr. Whattling," she ventured after he had apparently answered her earlier questions satisfactorily. "How have you been keeping yourself?"

The temptation was simply too great. "By gambling and horse racing, Madam," he replied. "I find throwing away a bundle on a fresh pony invigorating. I imagine that's what's landed me in the financial spot I'm in."

"So many gentlemen in financial difficulties these days," Mrs. Brighton commiserated. "What a blessing we do not have such a problem."

"I don't imagine anyone would have such difficulties were they in our shoes, Mama," Fanny replied with her characteristic laugh. "Why, I could gamble as long as I like and most likely I'd never do more than touch the interest. Do you hunt, Mr. Whattling?"

He had hunted any number of times, finding the pastime enjoyable with a good field. "Not a great deal," he replied. "Tedious sport."

He had the great satisfaction of seeing Mrs. Brighton frown. Fanny pursed her lips thoughtfully. "That will have to change, of course," she murmured. "I am quite fond of the sport."

"And I imagine you're quite good at it," Kevin responded, offering her his most charming smile and wondering just how soon he could get out of the house without insulting them both. However, as the questioning continued, he began to wonder whether he cared if he insulted them. He could not like the mercenary gleam in those pale blue eyes. The way she kept brushing against his coat as if to ascertain that the muscles she was seeing were real only made him want to quit the house in haste.

After another half hour, he managed to find his opening and bowed himself out with some excuse about seeing to his estates. He vowed never to return. Money or no money, he refused to be trotted out the rest of his life as the fine specimen of a man Fanny Brighton had bought. Jenny would never have treated him as if he were the strongest steer at auction!

But had he treated Eugennia any differently? he thought as he headed for his apartments. True, he hadn't patted her withers or demanded to count her teeth, but he certainly had gone in with the understanding of exactly what she was worth financially. He had sought to bargain his male prowess for her money, all the while hoping she might have more to offer than financial support. And she had considerably more to offer. Perhaps that was what had been bothering him. Instead of a straight bargain—his good looks for her fortune—he had been willing to take her spirit, her intelligence, and her beauty as well. It had never been an even bargain—the benefit was all his.

It was that subconscious realization, no doubt, that had given him his gray hair.

No, Eugennia Welch was well rid of him. The only question was—what was he to do now?

Eleven

Frowning, Giles lowered the day's *Times* to regard the thin packet his man was handing to him. "What is this?"

"The delivery boy said it was from Mr. Whattling, sir," Jacobs replied. "He didn't wait for a reply. Shall I send someone to ask Mr. Whattling?"

"No, that will be all." Giles waved him off. He set the paper aside on the teak table at his elbow, taking his feet off the leather-upholstered ottoman. Ripping open the packet, he saw inside two tickets to see Kean at Drury Lane for that night. The accompanying note read, "For all your support, Whattling."

Giles sighed, leaning back in his padded armchair. It was clear to him that Kevin was trying to make amends. But Kevin had signed the card Whattling, as opposed to the more brotherly Kevin that Giles had been calling him since they had gone to Eton together. And the angry scrawl was so unlike Kevin's usual writing. This could only mean that Kevin wasn't entirely over his fit of pique. Besides, the other ticket could only be for Nigel, and the fact that Kevin hadn't had it delivered to his friend's door clearly showed that Kevin wasn't willing to face him just yet.

This heiress business was tearing them apart! He had always hoped they'd each find pleasant young ladies to wed, if he could even bring himself to court one, and if

Nigel could bring himself to forget the one who had broken his heart before he had enlisted. Miss Welch, for all Giles's original objections, seemed as if she might be a good match for Kev. Why couldn't she be more reasonable? She was a bluestocking; why couldn't she see the logic of Kevin's courtship? Any way she cut it, Giles felt, she was getting a bargain. What kind of person passed up such a paragon as Kevin Whattling?

Still, he couldn't help but support Nigel's position as well. There did seem to be something dishonest about courting a woman simply because she possessed a large fortune. He felt it equally dishonest to court a woman simply because she was particularly lovely. A person should be valued for themselves. Heaven only knew, if he had been valued only for his face or fortune, he'd have had no friends at all!

However, it would have been uncharitable not to have accepted. He could hardly insult one of his truest and dearest friends. Besides, if he and Nigel went, perhaps they might find a way to make amends. Perhaps Kevin would be there smiling as usual, the tension between the three of them would evaporate, and things would be as they were before the infernal mess with Robbie. It was worth a try.

All he had to do now was convince Nigel.

George Safton sat in the center box of the Drury Lane theater, with near royalty in boxes at either side, smiling down at the poor fellows in the pit. Even without opera glasses, he could make out Giles Sloane's shock of red hair, front row, center. He could only hope that the gentleman next to him was Whattling, although the hair didn't seem quite right. He hadn't considered when he sent the two tickets that Sloane would assume the second ticket was for someone other than Whattling. In fact, he had counted on the fact that Sloane would go directly to Whattling, and Whattling would be so curious about the person impersonating him that he would come to the theater to investigate. George could only hope he had succeeded.

He smiled over at his companion, and Eugennia managed a smile back. He had also been hoping that her rather drab taste in clothing might improve for a theater outing, but the navy silk evening gown she wore was suited more to an elderly matron than a younger woman. True, the neckline plunged a bit more than her usual style, but it still failed to show the tops of her breasts, as did the more fashionable gowns of so many of the ladies around them. Nevertheless, the creamy skin revealed was a perfect setting for the sapphires that glittered at her throat. The necklace and matching earbobs would fetch a pretty price, and he could only hope that the appreciative gleam in his eye would be attributed to something other than the fact that he was calculating exactly how much.

Eugennia felt his continued gaze and turned her own steadfastly to the stage below. The intermission between acts had just begun, and she was sure he was expecting her to make conversation. If it had been Susan St. John or one of her other friends beside her, she was sure she would be able to think of something to say. Indeed, she wouldn't even have to work at it. But the man beside her was making her more and more uneasy.

She couldn't say what it was exactly that made her doubt him. Since the moment he had picked her and Martha up at her town house, he had been completely attentive and charming. One could scarcely complain about his spotless black evening wear, although she found she preferred the white waistcoat Kevin wore to George's black and white striped one.

As they left for the theater, George had made sure the ermine-trimmed lap robes were tucked around her and Martha, even though she hardly needed them in her navy velvet evening cloak. He had chatted pleasantly with them all the way through London, making Martha blush and giggle with his fulsome compliments. When they had arrived at the theater, he had ushered them up the sweeping stairs to what had to be the largest private box in the theater. She and Martha had never bothered to purchase such luxurious accommodations. She should have felt like a princess.

But his attentions only served to annoy her, perhaps because there didn't seem to be any logical reason for them. He hardly needed her fortune, if the opulent effects were any indication. He certainly wasn't interested in intelligent conversation—his talks with Martha routinely revolved around the weather, the latest fashion, or their neighbors' private affairs. And just as when Kevin had arrived on her doorstep, she could not credit that a Corinthian could want to be her friend. Besides, his charming smiles seemed strained to her, his laughter forced. She vowed she would simply make it through the evening and avoid any further dealings with him. If he should show up at her home again, she would simply tell Fiching not to receive him. She had had entirely enough of Corinthians.

Except that one Corinthian seemed to have invaded her thoughts. It certainly didn't help that the play tonight was *Hamlet;* she kept seeing Kevin in the brooding prince. But even earlier, when she had tried to read the book Susan had picked, she saw him in the characters, especially the dashing Willoughby. When she had tried to catch up on her correspondence with the Egyptian expedition she was sponsoring, she kept picturing him as a pharaoh, with female slaves at his beck and call, eager to do his bidding.

When she had attempted to classify the rare butterfly her entomologist colleague had given her, she caught herself wondering which of the many colors in its wings most closely resembled the blue in Kevin's eyes. If she had sent him packing to salvage her intellectual, orderly life, she had failed miserably.

The simple truth, she admitted to herself, was that she missed him terribly. She'd never realized how solitary her life was. How much more enjoyable it would have been to share her favorite pastimes with someone she admired and respected, better, with someone she loved. Yet, fearing that her emotions would override her reason, she had allowed herself to do exactly that and the result was that she had lost the chance fate had offered her. *I should have thought things through more carefully,* she scolded herself. She should have given herself more time to get used to the idea of being courted. She had behaved like a fool, a term she had never thought to apply to herself.

Yet, she realized, it wasn't entirely foolishness that had caused her to send him packing. She was afraid of him. His very presence threatened to change her whole way of life. Even though she had been wishing for such a change, its sudden advent had been too much for her. Craven, she had refused him. And it was too late to make amends. One did not give a Corinthian the cut direct and try to apologize afterward. She was very much afraid she would never see Kevin Whattling again.

Down in the pit, Giles nudged Nigel as the people around them stretched and chatted. "Do you see him?"

Nigel stood, putting his opera glasses to good use. "No. I think he would have joined us if he were in the pit. And there's no sign of him in any of the boxes. Hello, what's this?"

"What?" Giles demanded.

"Miss Welch, if I remember the lady correctly from our near miss in the park. And with Safton."

"Let me see," Giles gasped, grabbing the glasses. Nigel nodded in the general direction, then made a study of the floor while Giles trained the glasses toward the box. "By God, you're right, Nigel! What can this mean?"

"She's found someone who'll flatter her more," Nigel humphed. "Trust Safton to know how to address a lady's vanity."

Giles frowned, lowering the glasses. "I would have thought more of her. Bluestocking, you know. You'd think she'd see through such blatant cozening."

"Women see what they want," Nigel snapped. "Besides, if she had any intelligence whatsoever, she couldn't possibly prefer that viper to our Kevin."

"Of course," Giles agreed, raising the glasses again. "Nigel! Safton is leaving! Perhaps he was only visiting."

"Perhaps," Nigel allowed. "Although I still ask why."

Giles lowered the glasses again and shoved them at Nigel. "Now's our chance. We must warn her."

Nigel caught his arm as he made to leave. "Are you mad? She doesn't even know us. Why would she admit us to her box, let alone listen to us malign another gentleman?"

"But we can't leave her to Safton!" Giles wailed. "Would you let your sister be escorted by that cad? Your cousin?"

"I haven't a sister or female cousin, as you well know," Nigel protested, but Giles could tell he was weakening.

"Would you pass off an opera dancer you were done with to Safton?" Giles countered.

"Good God, no," Nigel shuddered. "But this is hardly the same thing."

Giles reddened as he realized the implication. "Well, no, of course not. But you ought to take my point. The lady probably doesn't get about much, and so cannot know Safton's reputation. Don't you see, Nigel, this is just like the situation with Robbie! We cannot let Safton ruin another life!"

Nigel sighed. "Point well taken, Giles. Very well. Lead on."

Giles scurried out of the row, and with Nigel following, hurried through the milling crowds in the lobby, up the stairs and down the corridor behind the boxes. He located the center box easily, then paused to square his shoulders before knocking.

Inside the box, Martha jumped to her feet at the sound of the knock. "Mr. Safton must have forgotten something," she cried, hurrying to answer.

Eugennia frowned, wondering what their escort could have forgotten that would prevent him from fetching some refreshments from below. Her frown deepened when she saw two unknown gentlemen in the doorway. While they looked quite presentable in their evening black, they appeared a somewhat mismatched set—one tall and angular with spare hair and features, and the other round as an orange, with hair to match. *I certainly seem to be attracting a rather curious set of admirers lately,* she thought.

"I'm very sorry to intrude on you like this," Giles murmured, finding his good intentions wilting under the glare from Miss Welch's guardian dragon and the frown from the lady herself. "I'm Mr. Giles Sloane, and this is Sir Nigel Dillingham. We, er, that is, I, er . . ."

"We're friends of Kevin Whattling's," Nigel announced, pushing past a startled Miss Tindale. "And we must speak to Miss Welch on a matter of some importance."

"Well, I never," Martha bridled.

Something in their attitude told Eugennia that she should listen to them.

"Let them in, Martha," she commanded. "I think you will want to thank Mr. Sloane. I believe he's the one who provided us with the excellent chocolate. Am I right, sir?"

Giles could feel himself blushing. "Yes, ma'am. A small token of appreciation I knew Mr. Whattling would want to make, if he could."

"Well, it was excellent chocolate," Martha allowed, returning to her seat and spreading the skirts of her black silk evening gown. "You may continue, Mr. Sloane."

"Thank you, Madam," he nodded to Miss Tindale. Then he turned his earnest gaze on Eugennia, but he couldn't seem to speak. His blush deepened, and he had to look at his companion for assistance.

"Giles felt it our duty to warn you, Madam," Nigel muttered obligingly. "We know you have rejected Kevin's suit, but—"

"But you can call him back if you like," Giles interrupted, odd light shining in his blue eyes. She wanted to take umbrage—imagine two strangers telling her how to direct her personal life—but something about Giles made her want to hear them out.

"Truly, Miss Welch," he was saying pleadingly, "he is a great gun. Kev and I have been friends since childhood, and I've never wanted for a better companion. He's always stood by me, when I was sick or needed someone to talk with. Ask Sir Nigel here—Kevin saved his life after he was mustered out of the Army and fell on dark times. Why, Nigel might have turned into a maudlin drunk if it weren't for Kev! Kev is kind, loyal, generous—well as generous as he can be of late—trustworthy—"

"That's enough, Giles," Nigel warned, face reddening in obvious embarrassment. "The man isn't dead and Miss Welch hardly asked you in to provide his eulogy."

Giles snapped his mouth shut, looking down at his feet in misery.

Eugennia's heart went out to him. "It is very noble of you to support your friend, Mr. Sloane. I sympathize with his plight, believe me. But you mustn't ask me to sacrifice my life for a man I scarcely know."

"No, indeed, Madam," Nigel nodded while Giles squirmed. "That is precisely why we're here. I may not be as eloquent as my friend Sloane, here, but I can only say that you've traded gold for dross."

Eugennia frowned. "I beg your pardon?"

"Your escort this evening, Madam—George Safton. He is a liar, a cheat, a murderer, and in no way a gentleman. You may have rid yourself of Kevin on good motives, but you haven't done yourself any favors by taking up with Safton."

Eugennia could feel herself growing redder with each word as her heart sped. Her intuition had been right! Safton was much worse than he seemed. Beside her, Martha was gaping in astonishment.

"I think, Sir Nigel," Eugennia managed, "that you had better explain yourself."

"Yes, Dillingham," Safton purred from the doorway. "Perhaps you'd better do just that."

Twelve

Giles moaned and sank onto the chair next to Miss Tindale. Nigel stiffened, and Eugennia swore his fists doubled at his sides before he clasped them behind his back.

"We were simply telling the lady that she should be careful how she picks her company," Nigel replied. "As I understand that the lady is exceptionally intelligent, we shouldn't have to say more. Give Mr. Safton his seat, Giles. The second act will be beginning shortly. Ladies, your servant."

Giles rose and swallowed. "Ladies."

Neither looked at Safton, who moved aside to let them exit. Eugennia couldn't let them leave without acknowledging their efforts. Based on Mr. Safton's reaction, and their own, they had risked much to warn her. Like the Kevin Whattling they both admired, Giles Sloane and Sir Nigel were obviously gentlemen of honor. Perhaps she had another chance after all.

"Mr. Sloane," she called. Giles stopped immediately. "Thank you for stopping by. If you should see our mutual friend, please let him know that my schedule has changed and I would be delighted to receive him any time this week. I hope you understand."

Giles beamed at her. "Yes, Miss Welch. I take your meaning. Thank you, thank you very much." He caught Safton glowering at him and ducked out into the corridor. Safton shut the door behind him.

He turned immediately to Eugennia. "Miss Welch, I apologize for leaving you. Once again London shows its degenerate side. I would have thought two ladies would be safe alone in a theater of this reputation. I hope nothing those two ruffians said frightened you."

"I hardly know what to make of it!" Martha gasped, fanning her face with her gloved hand. "Imagine anyone so bold!"

"You cannot blame them for supporting a friend," Eugennia put in. "Although I must say their manner left something to be desired. Mr. Safton, I am very glad you brought those drinks just then. I am parched."

He readily handed her the champagne goblet, turning to offer Miss Tindale the other. "Always at your service, Miss Welch. Are you sure you're all right?"

"I'm fine, I thank you," she replied, taking a sip. "Please don't trouble yourself. Oh look, there goes the curtain."

He returned to his seat as the lights dimmed. She sat beside him sipping the champagne as if nothing untoward had happened. He would not have thought she had it in her. Sloane and Dillingham's interference would surely have troubled her more than she indicated. His own standing was clearly in jeopardy. He turned his gaze on the stage, but he hardly saw the play. So, Whattling hadn't been here to witness George's triumph, and Sloane and Dillingham had managed to get her to allow Whattling to call again. George could feel his grip on the situation loosening. He would have to rethink his options. Which would be more expeditious—to continue cozening Miss Welch, or to try some other way to gain Whattling's company?

He watched Eugennia's profile lit by the lights from the

We'd Like to Invite You to Subscribe to Zebra's Regency Romance Book Club and Give You a Gift of 4 Free Books as Your Introduction! (Worth $19.96!)

If you're a Regency lover, imagine the joy of getting 4 FREE Zebra Regency Romances and then the chance to have these lovely stories delivered to your home each month at the lowest prices available! Well, that's our offer to you and here's how you benefit by becoming a Zebra Home Subscription Service subscriber:

- **4 FREE** Introductory Regency Romances are delivered to your doorstep

- 4 BRAND NEW Regencies are then delivered each month (usually before they're available in bookstores)

- Subscribers save almost $4.00 every month

- Home delivery is always **FREE**

- You also receive a **FREE** monthly newsletter, *Zebra/ Pinnacle Romance News* which features author profiles, contests, subscriber benefits, book previews and more

- No risks or obligations...in other words you can cancel whenever you wish with no questions asked

Join the thousands of readers who enjoy the savings and convenience offered to Regency Romance subscribers. After your initial introductory shipment, you receive 4 brand-new Zebra Regency Romances each month to examine for 10 days. Then, if you decide to keep the books, you'll pay the preferred subscriber's price of just $4.00 per title. That's only $16.00 for all 4 books and there's never an extra charge for shipping and handling.

It's a no-lose proposition, so return the FREE BOOK CERTIFICATE today!

Say Yes to 4 Free Books!
Complete and return the order card to receive this $19.96 value, ABSOLUTELY FREE!

(If the certificate is missing below, write to:)
Zebra Home Subscription Service, Inc.,
120 Brighton Road, P.O. Box 5214, Clifton, New Jersey 07015-5214
or call TOLL-FREE 1-888-345-BOOK

FREE BOOK CERTIFICATE

YES! Please rush me 4 Zebra Regency Romances without cost or obligation. I understand that each month thereafter I will be able to preview 4 brand-new Regency Romances FREE for 10 days. Then, if I should decide to keep them, I will pay the money-saving preferred subscriber's price of just $16.00 for all 4...that's a savings of almost $4 off the publisher's price with no additional charge for shipping and handling. I may return any shipment within 10 days and owe nothing, and I may cancel this subscription at any time. My 4 FREE books will be mine to keep in any case.

Name _____

Address _____ Apt. _____

City _____ State _____ Zip _____

Telephone ( ) _____

Signature _____ RG0599
(If under 18, parent or guardian must sign.)

Terms and prices subject to change. Orders subject to acceptance by Zebra Home Subscription Service, Inc.

stage below. The jewels glinted at her throat. No, there was a great deal he could accomplish here. Even if he didn't get the lady and Whattling to part company, there might be a way he could get her to part company with the sapphires, and anything else to which he took a fancy. He'd have to carefully consider the best way to proceed. Whatever happened, Miss Eugennia Welch wasn't going to leave his grip before he got what he wanted.

In the lobby, Giles was in transports. "Did you hear that, Nigel! She's willing to forgive him! We must find Kevin and tell him at once."

"Easy, old boy," Nigel cautioned, catching him by the edge of his coat. "We have no idea where Kevin is at the moment, and Miss Welch can hardly receive him before tomorrow afternoon anyway. I have no interest in this tedious drama, but you can't expect me to go trundling all about town. Let's go home and tell him in the morning."

But Giles was not to be deterred. As Nigel had seldom seen him so insistent, he decided that it was the better part of valor to give in. They tried White's, Watier's, and several other private clubs, to no avail. Midnight found them at Kevin's door, although they scarcely expected him to answer their knock, and in his nightshirt.

"Are you ill?" Nigel demanded when he had let them in, going to light a lamp.

Kevin yawned as the wick flared. "Not in the slightest. Can't a man get a good night's sleep without someone thinking he's in his dotage?"

"Of course," Nigel humphed. "It simply isn't like you, that's all."

Kevin shrugged. "Well, perhaps you don't know me as well as you thought. Now, what is it that brings you rapping at my door unannounced?"

Giles was fairly hopping in his desire to tell. "She wants you back, Kevin. She said so herself."

"What are you talking about?" Kevin frowned, glancing between the two of them. "Who wants me back?"

"Miss Welch," Nigel put in. "Hard to credit, I know, since she is supposed to be remarkably perceptive, but there you have it."

"Perhaps you'd better explain, slowly," Kevin murmured, afraid to hope. "You say you saw Jen, er Miss Welch? And she said something about me?"

" 'If you should see our mutual friend,' " Giles quoted helpfully, " 'please let him know that my schedule has changed and I would be delighted to receive him any time this week.' "

Nigel looked impressed. "I say, well done, Giles."

Kevin ran his hand back through his hair. Could it be true? Was she willing to take a chance on him after all? "When did this happen? Where?"

"We were at Drury Lane," Giles explained excitedly, "in the pit, using those tickets you sent us and—"

"Tickets?" Kevin demanded. "What tickets?"

Giles smile faded. "You remember. You sent them to my house with a note. I assumed they were for Nigel and me."

"I sent no tickets," Kevin assured him. "I don't suppose you kept the note."

Giles shook his head. "No. I saw no reason to. But I don't understand. The note was signed with your name, Kev. Who would do such a thing?"

"Who indeed?" Kevin mused. "The same someone who sent flowers to Miss Welch, I warrant."

"But we sent the flowers," Giles protested. "We told you."

"You sent roses," Kevin corrected him. "So you told me.

Someone else sent lilies, gardenias, and carnations the same day."

Nigel wrinkled his nose. "Place must have stunk. No wonder she tossed you out."

"But she wants you back now," Giles insisted. "So whoever is behind all this must be trying to help."

"I wonder," Kevin murmured. "Have either of you told anyone else about my predicament?"

Giles and Nigel exchanged glances. Nigel cleared his throat. "Of course not, old man, but we didn't have to. It's well known about town that you've pockets to let. Could be any number of people trying to help you without your knowing it."

"But if they're helping *me,* why send tickets to you and Giles? It must be someone well known to the three of us. Did you see anyone else at the theater you knew?"

Again they exchanged glances. This time their look chilled his blood.

"Tell me," Kevin demanded.

Giles shook his head.

"I'll do it," Nigel snapped. "We saw Safton. He was escorting Miss Welch."

"What!" Kevin's cry made both his friends start. "And you left her there with him?"

"Easy," Nigel cautioned, putting a hand on his arm. "We warned the lady first. If she's as bright as everyone says she is, she'll know what to do."

"And she had her companion with her," Giles put in, although he paused to chew his lower lip before continuing. "I don't suppose anything bad could happen with her there, could it?"

Kevin took a deep breath. "No, not tonight. Thanks to you, George will be careful not to show his hand just yet. I want him away from her before he can finish whatever nasty little game he's playing." The arrogant handwriting on the one note appeared in his mind's eye again, and he struck his fist against his palm. "That's it! The notes are from Safton! They must be!"

"But why?" Nigel demanded. "As Giles pointed out, the notes were connected to events designed to help you. I can't see Safton wanting to help anyone, especially you."

"I know it doesn't make much sense," Kevin agreed, "but I'd wager what little I have left that I'm right. He's playing some deep game, the kind he loves most, and Eugennia will be the loser if we aren't careful. Much as I'd like to catch him in the act, we must stop him before he hurts anyone."

Nigel and Giles nodded.

Kevin rose. "Thank you, gentlemen, for your continued assistance. I don't think I need to tell you that I am much indebted to you." He laughed suddenly. "Actually, I'm less in debt to you than I am to most people, but what's a few thousand pounds between friends." He offered them his hand, and they shook it in turn, returning his grin. "I shall call on Miss Welch tomorrow. Who knows, perhaps there's still a chance that she'll be the bluestocking on my knee."

If it hadn't been for Giles and Nigel's mention of Safton, Kevin had to admit, he probably wouldn't have called on Eugennia, even though she had given him leave to do so. He had just finished convincing himself that she was well off without his courtship. He didn't intend to continue it even to displace the odious Safton. Of course, he wasn't sure what he was going to do about his debts. Leaving for the Continent was actually starting to look appealing. All the more reason to do something worthwhile with his remaining time. He arrived on her doorstep at the unfashionable hour of eleven.

Only to be told she was not at home.

The elderly butler Fiching was adamant. "I'm very sorry, Mr. Whattling. She really didn't tell me not to admit you. It's just that she's started on one of her studies again, and she dragged poor Miss Tindale off to some booksellers this morning. There's no telling when she'll be back. You won't credit how long it takes her to find the information she wants sometimes!"

"I don't suppose you'd let me wait?" Kevin had asked, without much hope of positive response. To his surprise, Fiching had been only too happy to show him into the saffron sitting room, leaving him there with the promise of tea and cakes.

Kevin tried perching on the white sofa, but he found he had too much energy to simply sit calmly and wait. He tried pacing about the room, but the decorative tables and glass cabinets were arranged so that he couldn't get a good stride going. Frustrated, he paused to frown at one of the cases. His frown changed to a look of wonder as he began to recognize what he was seeing.

The case he was gazing into held ancient artifacts of some kind; he'd warrant Egyptian if his brief glimpses of the Elgin marbles were any indication. There was a rough-edged stone tablet with strange, indecipherable lettering carved into its face, an insect with wings of onyx set in a body of lapis, and the bust of a woman who strongly resembled a cat. Fascinated, he moved to another cabinet, to find it full of butterflies, each painstakingly mounted and labeled with a fine hand. He moved to the third cabinet and saw it crowded with books, some very old if he were any judge. One stood open on a shelf, a satin bookmark holding the reader's place.

"A Midsummer Night's Dream," Eugennia said softly in the doorway. "It's one of my favorite plays by the Bard."

"Mine as well," he replied, steeling himself to turn and look at her. "But somehow I always thought my courting would go more smoothly."

She was dressed in a brown satin pelisse that somehow made her look frail. Something about her face told him she had been crying recently. He had an overwhelming desire to find out who had caused it and beat him senseless.

She smiled at him, and the sun came out. "How nice to see you again, Mr. Whattling. Am I to take it that my message got through?"

He bowed. "It did indeed. Giles is a reliable postman. And I am your eternal servant."

She narrowed her eyes. "I would much sooner have a friend."

"You have one. If you ever need anything, you have only to ask."

The intensity of his response brought a blush to her cheek. "I was hoping that perhaps you might be willing to continue where we left off."

Was she telling him that she wanted him to continue courting her? He could scarcely credit it. And he still wasn't sure it was the best thing for her. "We can discuss that if you like, Madam. I came today on more urgent business."

"Oh?" she frowned, but before he could elaborate, Fiching bustled in to take her pelisse and Miss Tindale hurried into the room to take up her post as chaperone. Kevin sighed. It wasn't going to be easy.

"You were saying, Mr. Whattling?" she asked as she was seated on the white sofa. Miss Tindale had taken up residence in the chair nearby, eyeing him in a distinctly doubtful fashion. Annoyed, he plunked himself down as close to Eugennia as was polite under the circumstances. Miss Tindale glowered.

"Mr. Sloane and Sir Nigel mentioned your escort last night," he began. She bridled immediately, and the hair on Miss Tindale's mole stood out accusingly. He tried to soften his approach. "I'm very glad you were able to enjoy the performance."

Miss Tindale relaxed and took up her needlework.

"In truth, I did not enjoy it much at all," Eugennia murmured beside him. "I thought Mr. Safton was a particular friend of yours, Mr. Whattling, but even before your other friends came to warn me, I felt there is something about him that disturbed me."

He wanted to rejoice at her good sense, but the thought that Safton had used him to get close to her incensed him. It was too much like what had happened to Robbie. "I want to assure you, Miss Welch, that George Safton is no friend of mine."

Miss Tindale's head came up, and Eugennia regarded him wide-eyed. "But he said he knew you."

"He knows me. There was a time, a very brief time, in which I thought of him as a companion. I mistakenly believed him a gentleman, a fellow Corinthian. He is neither of those things. George Safton is a creature who preys upon those innocent enough to be taken in by his charming manner and handsome facade. When Giles and Nigel told me he was with you, I came as soon as I could."

"A likely story," Miss Tindale sniffed. "Honestly, Eugennia, how can you sit there and let him malign so fine a gentleman as Mr. Safton? It's plain to see that he's just jealous."

Eugennia started. Jealous? She glanced at Kevin quickly, but he was frowning at Miss Tindale as if he very much wanted to bite off her long nose. If he was jealous, did that mean he had some feeling for her? Or was it merely one charming rake protecting his game from another?

"I won't deny that the thought of any man but me escorting Miss Welch troubles me," Kevin replied sharply. "But that doesn't change what George Safton is." He turned to Eugennia. "Surely you've seen through him, Miss Welch. Your statement earlier is proof of that. Didn't you say that something about him bothers you?"

"Humpf," Miss Tindale answered. "Any charming gentleman bothers her. She didn't much like you either."

He winced at the thought that Jenny might have lumped him in the same category as Safton.

"That's enough, Martha," Eugennia said firmly. "It doesn't matter what you think of Mr. Safton or Mr. Whattling. I'm the one that's being courted, if you please."

"He's courting you!" Kevin felt his hands tremble in his desire to throttle Safton for even thinking about touching Jenny Welch. "The bounder! I'll see him shot on the Commons!"

"Ha, you see!" Martha chortled. "Jealous, just like I said."

"Martha," Eugennia snapped, "leave us."

Kevin froze. Miss Tindale stared at her mistress. "But Jenny, you can't be left alone with—"

"I can be left alone with an old friend who wishes a private word. Fiching, escort Miss Tindale into the library. I'll call if I need assistance."

Kevin laid a hand on her arm even as Miss Tindale slowly rose to her feet, face white. "She's right, you know. I'm not worth your reputation."

"I'll be the judge of that," Eugennia declared with a toss of her head. She could hear her heart thundering in her ears, but she glared at Fiching, who jumped forward and took Martha's arm. Martha sniffed and shuffled from the room. Fiching closed the door behind her.

"I think we should come to an agreement," she told him, although she found it impossible to look at him. "You evaded my question earlier. Are you still interested in courting me?"

She said it with such defiance, but he would have had to have been blind not to see how much his answer meant to her. Something inside him snapped, and he felt his heart beating for the first time in a long time. "Nothing would give me more pleasure," he assured her.

Her cheeks reddened, but she continued with a firm voice. "I cannot promise you my answer. I do not know my own mind. But I've enjoyed our time together, and I have been calling myself a fool for sending you off for no better reason than that I was afraid."

"Afraid?" he frowned. "I assure you, Miss Welch, I am no George Safton. You have nothing to fear from me."

She raised her head and looked at him at last, eyes solemn. "On the contrary, Mr. Whattling. I have nothing to fear from Mr. Safton because I have good friends like you to prevent me from being taken in. But I have everything to fear from you because the only thing between you and me is my heart, and that, I fear, is entirely unreliable where you are concerned."

Thirteen

Nigel could not understand why Giles was not more pleased with himself when they met at White's again that night.

"But I thought your man said Kevin was smiling when he left her house," he grumbled at Giles's lackluster accounting of the day's events. "You were demmed interfering, if you ask me, but you were effective. I don't understand why you persist in pouting."

"I am not pouting," Giles protested, lips set in something remarkably resembling a pout. "I simply cannot feel we have done our full duty in this situation."

"Don't see why not," Nigel complained. "We sent flowers, you plied her with chocolate, we lowered ourselves to warn her off Safton. And you praised Kevin so much in her hearing one would think you were the one he was courting."

Giles colored. "Do you think anything I said untrue? Or do you not remember how Kevin and I found you?"

Now it was Nigel's turn to color. "You needn't remind me. I was in the very worst condition. Never thought I'd be fit for anything in life but military duty, then a lucky shot on the Peninsula and I'm sent home permanently. And I don't even limp!"

"No, you don't, which is a blessing," Giles remarked.

"And you found that there were others who would enjoy your company even if we weren't in your unit, didn't you?"

"Certainly, certainly. You and Kevin have been the best friends a man could ask for. But I don't generally go around spouting your virtues to every female you make eyes at."

"Malign me all you like," Giles replied, head high. "I know what I did was right. I only regret I didn't act sooner."

"Now do not harp on that chord again either," Nigel growled. "I agree with you that we were negligent in our duty as far as Robbie was concerned. I simply do not see how you think we can do more now. The man is dead!"

Giles eyed him, breast heaving as he struggled to put his thoughts into words. Nigel had known him too long to have to wait.

"Don't tell me," he sighed. "You think we should go after Safton."

Giles nodded vigorously in his relief not to have to say it aloud.

Nigel shook his head. "Are you daft, man? You know as well as I do the magistrates were unable to convict him of any wrongdoing in the matter of Robbie's death. What more can we do?"

"He has other suspicious activities," Giles protested. "He will slip up again. If we watch him, Nigel, we could be there in time to get the goods on him."

Nigel snorted. "That could take months, years! I do not see how that helps Kevin or Miss Welch."

"Perhaps it doesn't," Giles acknowledged, gaze lowered to the tabletop. "But it will help me come to terms with my inability to help poor Robbie. You do not have to come along, Nigel. I'll do it alone if I must."

"As if I'd let you face danger alone," Nigel grumbled.

Giles raised his gaze to beam at him.

"Do not crow just yet," Nigel snapped. "I may not be the best campaigner to retire from His Majesty's service, but I did earn my title honestly. We need a plan of attack, my lad. Safton will not be easy to catch. You might as well order us some dinner. I have a feeling this will take some time."

Kevin felt absurdly pleased with himself after his meeting with Eugennia. Not only had he succeeded in convincing her to send Safton packing, but she had admitted to having some feeling for him! It was more than he had expected and more than he deserved. If she wanted him, he would persevere and win her hand in marriage. He promised himself to be the very best of husbands so that she would never regret the price of her marriage.

Eugennia was just as pleased with the meeting. Martha continued to grumble, and it was hard to ignore Fiching's gloating grin every time she did. Eugennia was sure of her decision. The one good thing about George Safton's brief presence was that it had showed her what a true fortune hunter was like. Whatever Kevin Whattling was, he was honest. Time enough to find out if all the other traits Giles Sloane had attributed to him were real.

True to her plan, she instructed Fiching to tell Safton she wasn't at home. Fiching reported doing so that very afternoon, and that the man had been rather pleasant about the whole thing. She imagined he'd try to call again at some point, but he would eventually get the message. By then, she would either be married to Kevin Whattling or retired from this social whirl. Either way, she would be immune to George Safton's influence.

The last thing she expected when she, Martha, and Stevens set out the next morning on her constitutional down Curzon Street was to find George Safton waiting at the corner. She should have realized that he knew her habits—after all that was how they had met to begin with. But she hadn't imagined that he'd be there, for all the world like a panther lying in wait for a docile herd of antelope.

She saw him leaning against the lamppost several yards before they got there. Tempting as it was to simply turn around and go home, something told her it would be unwise to give him so direct a cut. Besides, she refused to be driven from her daily activities by some gentleman who was too dense to know when he wasn't wanted. Instead, she squared her shoulders and proceeded to the corner. Martha continued beside her, oblivious, but Eugennia took some comfort in Steven's wide shoulders and considerable bulk behind her.

Safton straightened and doffed his top hat, bowing, as she approached. He was dressed in his usual black, making him look just a little menacing. She heard Martha suck in a breath. Fiching must have instructed Stevens, for he stood a little taller, usually blank brown eyes narrowing.

"Miss Welch," Safton smiled charmingly. "How fortuitous. I had been hoping to encounter you."

"Mr. Safton," she nodded coolly, "I'm sure you were."

He raised a dark eyebrow. "Why Miss Welch, you seem a bit short with me today. Have I done something to displease you?"

Beside her, Martha was vigorously shaking her head no. Eugennia decided that roundaboutation would afford her nothing. "Mr. Safton, you were very kind to escort me home after that unfortunate incident the other day, and to see Miss Tindale and I to the theater the other night. But I'm afraid we've had some rather distressing reports about you, and I'm sure you'll understand that I am loath to continue our connection."

"I can surely understand," he said, handsome face showing obvious distress, "but Miss Welch, may I say it is unlike someone of your good sense to take gossip so seriously. Surely you understand how the ton can take delight in slandering one's reputation, belittling one's accomplishments?"

She understood all too well. Normally his comment would have won the day, but she couldn't shake off Kevin's unflinching dislike of the man, despite the fact that Martha was biting her lip beside her, obviously taken in. "If that is the case, I'm very sorry for you, Mr. Safton. But I must stand by my decision."

He looked perplexed. "But I have been completely aboveboard with you, have I not?"

"In most respects, Mr. Safton, you have," she allowed, but found she could not leave it at that. "However, twice now you have mentioned your supposed friendship with Mr. Whattling. Mr. Whattling tells me you are not his friend."

He drew himself up, clutching his breast. "What? Have I wounded him as well? Why hasn't he told me so himself?"

Eugennia could not stand the theatrics another minute. She turned away, tugging Martha with her. "I cannot say. You will have to talk to him yourself. Suffice it to say that you and I will not be meeting again. Goodbye, Mr. Safton."

"Wait!" He pushed in front of her, and she caught a

quick glimpse of a face contorted with rage before his pleasant smile disposed it. The glimpse sent a chill up her spine and she stepped back. He caught her hand.

"Please, Miss Welch, you must not listen to the stories you hear about me. I have been much maligned by my enemies. I assure you, I thought Mr. Whattling was my friend. It amazes me to hear he does not think so. But that has nothing do to with the friendship you and I have been building. I have so enjoyed our time together. Do not cut me off now."

Martha nudged her. "Listen to him, Eugennia," she hissed. "Does that sound like the villain Mr. Whattling painted?"

Eugennia ignored her. "I'm very sorry, Mr. Safton. I must do as I see fit. However, if you reconcile with Mr. Whattling and he informs me of the fact, I would be happy to receive you again. If Kevin is such a friend of yours, this shouldn't be a problem."

His grip on her hand tightened, and she tried to pull it back, alarm growing. Stevens took a step forward, but something about Safton's manner made him hesitate. The smile on Safton's face was a tight mask as he leaned closer and she saw the dangerous glint in his dark eyes. "I hope you'll reconsider, Miss Welch. I wouldn't want to count you among my enemies."

The malignant gaze was nearly hypnotizing, but the grip was becoming painful. "Let go of me, now," she told him quietly. "I don't think you want a scene."

"You have no idea what I want," he replied, but he broke off his hold and patted her shoulder.

"I'll abide by your wishes, of course, my dear Miss Welch. But you mustn't say I didn't warn you. Good day to you, and you, Miss Tindale." He nodded and strolled back around the corner, the crowds on Park Lane thankfully swallowing him up almost immediately.

Eugennia shook herself. "Martha, you will do me the honor of not mentioning that man in my hearing again. You are not to let him in the house; you are not to speak to him on the street. If I find that you have done so, I will sack you, despite all your years of service and the fact that I consider you a dear friend. You have been completely wrong about him, and I will brook no argument. Do I make myself clear?"

Martha swallowed, her pale, long nose trembling. "Yes, Miss Welch."

Eugennia put an arm about her waist and hugged her. "It's Jenny, you wretch, as you well know. And I adore you, but that man is dangerous, and you must heed me."

Miss Tindale nodded, sniffing back a tear. "But he seemed so presentable."

"The devil usually does," Eugennia told her, steering her back toward home, Stevens falling into step behind her. "How else do you think he entices souls? No one goes willingly to hell."

Miss Tindale shivered, but kept walking. None of them looked back.

So, Whattling had won, George fumed, stalking up Park Lane to where his carriage stood waiting. The lady was cutting George off while encouraging Kevin's suit. Not only was George losing his opportunity to thwart Kevin; he had lost the opportunity to part Miss Welch from any piece of her considerable fortune. Even if Kevin decided to spend some of it himself, he would hardly do so to George's benefit. The situation was simply unacceptable.

He would have to find another way. If he could not win Kevin's companionship, perhaps he could at least discredit him. If George could not stop the biting accusations, he could at least ensure they had no teeth. If he watched how the situation unfolded with Whattling and the bluestocking, surely he would find another opportunity to gain the upper hand. He would let them think the game was theirs, for now.

Fourteen

Kevin was determined to never again allow Eugennia the luxury of an entire day to rethink her response to his courting. He had already been skirting the edges of propriety to call daily. There wasn't much additional possible damage he could do if he increased their contact even more, and he might get Jenny to agree even sooner. With this in mind, he went the following afternoon with the express purpose of getting her to agree to accompany him to the theater that very evening. He wasn't sure of his reception, but he was a little surprised to find Jenny and Miss Tindale ensconced in the library, several open books piled about them, Miss Tindale taking notes while Eugennia dictated as she read.

"Pardon me, ladies," he called from the doorway in wonderment. "Is it safe to enter?"

Eugennia smiled up at him, closing the book with a snap. "Ah, the Corinthian arrives. Just in time, sir. We have questions."

"Oh?" he replied, not sure he wanted to come any closer with that odd light in her eyes. "About what?"

"Boxing," she responded, rising. "However, as we've been at this most of the morning, I'm getting a bit tired. Martha, would you care for lemonade?"

Martha rose eagerly. "That would be delightful."

Eugennia nodded, coming around the desk. "Excellent. Mr. Whattling, will you join us in the sitting room?"

He bowed her out in front of him along with Miss Tindale and followed them across the hall, still wondering. She sent the footman for refreshments and spread her gray lustring skirts to sit on one of the armchairs. Miss Tindale collapsed into her usual seat near the fireplace. Kevin relaxed on the white sofa.

"You had mentioned you boxed," Eugennia ventured. "Isn't that right?"

He nodded. "Yes, I have studied the art."

Her eyes lit up. "A student. Excellent. Ah, there you are, Fiching. That was quick."

"Yes, Madam," Fiching nodded, rolling the cart to her side. "Will there be anything else?"

She waved him out and began pouring immediately. Martha perked up as she handed her her glass. Eugennia couldn't help noticing Kevin frowning as she handed him his.

"Is something amiss, Mr. Whattling? Do you not care for lemonade?"

He shook his head. "Lemonade is delightful, I assure you. And nothing is particularly amiss. I seem to be having a difficult time concentrating in your presence." There, he had made the problem sound like a compliment, and he felt rather pleased with himself.

She missed the innuendo. "Why is that, do you think?"

Kevin took a sip on the pretense of pondering the answer. "I suspect I may be trying overly hard to impress you today."

"Why would you try harder today than any other day?" she asked with a frown; then her brow cleared and she blushed. "Oh, yes, I'd forgotten about our conversation yesterday."

Kevin set his lemonade down in mock annoyance. "Madam, if you can so easily forget my purpose in calling, I'm obviously doing something wrong."

Eugennia looked flustered and attempted to regain her composure by focusing on pouring lemonade into her own glass. "I am sorry, Mr. Whattling. You see, I've settled on a new course of study, and I'm afraid that sometimes seems to drive all other matters from my mind. If it doesn't offend you, could we converse today on the topic of boxing?"

"If you insist," Kevin sighed, still a bit put out. "Although I cannot credit that you really want to hear about it."

"Oh, but I do!" she assured him eagerly.

"Humor her, Mr. Whattling," Miss Tindale sniffed. "As she said, she's pursuing one of her studies again. We find it best to simply comply with her requests."

Kevin frowned. She made it sound as if Jenny was some candidate for Bedlam! He glanced at Jenny, only to find her hazel eyes alight with interest, gazing at him as if he alone held the answer to life's mysteries. If she wanted him to prose on about boxing, boxing it would be. "Very well, Madam. Where would you like me to begin?"

"Martha and I undertook a trip to the booksellers yesterday morning, and we procured several excellent texts. Mr. Milson at the lending library recommended *A Treatise Upon the Useful Science of Defense* by John Godfrey. After comparing it to the clippings Fiching had saved from the Boxiana series, however, I must say I find Mr. Egan more enlightening."

"Indeed," Kevin nodded, wondering how much she could possibly have learned about boxing by reading about it.

"Oh, yes," she continued earnestly. "I think I understand how a match is staged, the umpires and the seconds, as well as the kneemen and bottlemen. And the timing of rounds and breaks. As for the actual fighting, I believe I have grasped the rudimentary elements there as well." She ticked them off on her fingers. "There is the jab, the swing, the upper cut, and the, ah, Martha?"

"I think it was the cross," Martha supplied, but her frown indicated her hesitancy.

"Yes, of course, the cross. Right and left, I believe. How does that compare with your studies, Mr. Whattling?"

"I . . . I'm not sure," Kevin managed. Apparently one could learn a great deal by reading. He'd have to find a copy of those Egan articles; he thought perhaps Giles had mentioned them. Through reading them, it was as if she understood the sport better than Kevin did, and he had learned at the fists of Gentleman Jackson himself! "You appear to have made an excellent assessment, Miss Welch," he told her.

She nodded and took a sip of lemonade. "Good. What I wish to know next is, how does one know which tactic to use?"

"Well," Kevin replied thoughtfully, "I suppose I cannot speak for all gentlemen who box. As you mentioned, boxing is more of an art than a science, and each artist, if you will, goes about it in a different manner. Myself, I like to keep well back for a while and watch my opponent. Most often you'll see a pattern emerge. This one prefers to lead with his left, perhaps. Another throws his right shoulder forward just before jabbing. I use their weakness to determine the appropriate attack and defense."

"Fascinating," Eugennia breathed. "How many matches have you had?"

"True matches? None. I'm not a professional, Miss Welch. But matches between other hobbyists like myself, perhaps a dozen."

"And your record?"

He began to feel as if he were in school and being quizzed by the headmaster. "I've won ten."

She raised her eyebrows. "That sounds remarkably good. Why did you lose the two?"

He smiled at the memory. "One was to Gentleman Jackson. You'll have read of him, I suppose?"

"John Jackson of London," Eugennia replied readily. "He had three fights before retiring. He beat the Birmingham Giant Fewterell, lost to George The Brewer Ingelston, and won the championship from Mendoza. He runs an establishment at 13 Old Bond Street, I believe. The Pugilistic Club?"

"That's right," Kevin nodded, again amazed by her knowledge. "Though it's hard to boil down a man to a fight record. Lord Byron calls him the Professor of Pugilism. Lord Lowther had him put on a pugilistic fete for the Emperor of Russia last summer. It's safe to say that a good many gentlemen would never have learned to box if it weren't for Gentleman Jackson."

"Make a note of that, Martha," Jenny put in. "Please continue, Mr. Whattling."

Miss Tindale rolled her eyes, but Kevin wasn't sure why. Still, he complied with Jenny's request. "The Gentleman had been tutoring me for some time and felt I was ready to spar against him. I wasn't. Mayhap I'll never be. But it was a heady experience to fight him just the same."

"I would imagine. And the other bout you lost?"

He blinked and looked away from her. "The other does not signify. He was only a gentleman like myself. He has since left the ring. Did you have other questions?"

Puzzled by his response, she decided not to probe. "Well, really only one, but I think I've seen the answer already. There are other sports less brutal. Why do you box?"

Now he raised his eyebrows. "Why box?"

"Yes. Why?"

Miss Tindale shuddered. "It does seem so very blood-thirsty."

Kevin rose and attempted to pace the room, moving among the tables and glass cases. He didn't want Eugennia thinking he was some beast who derived pleasure from beating others. George Safton sprang immediately to mind, and he thrust the thought just as quickly away. "An interesting question, Miss Welch," he allowed. "I never really considered it before." He paused to eye her. "Yet you said you saw an answer in my earlier conversation."

She felt herself blush. "Yes. In your face. You obviously enjoy it, much as I enjoy my studies. To you, it is an art. You studied at the feet of a master and you long to try your hand with the same skill. I do not understand why striking another person should be considered art, but I'm sure there is skill involved, as in any sport. I would say you are very good at it. You have worked to make yourself so."

"Uncanny," Kevin breathed, sinking back onto the sofa. His blue eyes were intent on her face, and she felt the blush deepen. "You gathered all that from our brief conversation? Madam, you astonish me!"

Miss Tindale beamed at him, and he realized she was tremendously proud of Eugennia's insight as well.

"Oh, it is nothing," Eugennia waved the praise away, feeling embarrassed. "I am no seer. Anyone seeing you could understand your feelings for the sport."

"Not everyone," he replied, and she was surprised by the bitterness in his tone. She looked at him askance, but he had risen once again to return to his pacing. She glanced at Martha, who motioned her forward with a wave of her crystal glass. Jenny squared her shoulders to push the conversation in the direction she really wanted it to go.

"Do you think I might view a match?"

Kevin paused, frowning. "As Miss Tindale implied, Miss Welch, it is hardly a sport for ladies."

"You see," Miss Tindale put in with determination. "Even Mr. Whattling agrees with me in that regard. I pray you will listen to him for once, Eugennia."

"Pishposh," Eugennia snapped. "My sensibilities are not so refined as to be appalled by a bit of blood. Two years ago I watched a surgeon perform, if you will remember, Martha. Besides, not all matches end in bloodshed, do they, Mr. Whattling?"

"No," he murmured, thinking of one match that had. "But one never knows the outcome. The gentleman I mentioned earlier, the one who beat me in a sparring match, was unexpectedly killed in another match. I would prefer you to stay away from boxing, Miss Welch."

Eugennia frowned. She could understand his reluctance after such an experience, but she wasn't used to anyone but Martha protesting her studies. "I do not see how I can properly study the sport if I never actually view it in action."

"Precisely why you should not study it at all," put in Miss Tindale. "Studying the cut of men's coats last year was bad enough. Studying boxing is decidedly unladylike."

Jenny glanced between Martha's determined scowl and Kevin's pale frown. She was quite immune to Martha's protests, but something told her she should try to understand Kevin's concern.

"Thank you for your concern, Martha," she murmured.

"Perhaps it would be best if I confined my studies to books for the moment. I wonder if you'd mind going upstairs for those articles by Mr. Egan. I believe I left them on my bedside table. If not, they're in the sewing room. And if you don't find them there, pray check the library."

Martha frowned, glancing between the two of them, and Kevin tried not to grin in triumph as he realized he was to have a moment alone with Jenny. Martha must have realized it as well, for with a humph, she quit the room.

Kevin moved to stand beside Eugennia. She gazed up at him, trying to decide how to begin.

"And what confidences do you have for me today, my dear?" he asked, half teasing.

He suddenly seemed a bit too close, towering as he did over her. She scooted back as far as the wing-backed chair would allow. "Nothing of great import, sir. I sensed your concern about my interest in boxing, and I thought you might feel more comfortable speaking your mind if Miss Tindale were gone."

So he was the one who was supposed to offer confidences. He couldn't think of anything he should say, Miss Tindale or no Miss Tindale. He still couldn't easily converse about Robbie's death. Besides, he rather liked the fact that his nearness was obviously discomposing Jenny. He had a thirty-second boxing match with his conscience, and his desire to have her next to him won. He took her hand and pulled her to her feet before him. "And why should a bluestocking care what a Corinthian thinks? I would guess that a word of concern from my lips would hardly be enough to dissuade you from your intellectual pursuits."

His words only made her aware of how close his lips were to her own. "Quite . . . quite right," she stammered. This was not at all what she had had in mind. She was losing control of the situation. And he was entirely too close. However, her attempts to move away only brought her up against the refreshment cart, which rattled alarmingly. She stumbled, and he caught her in his arms in the pretense of preventing her fall.

Jenny gazed up at him, frozen in his arms. She could feel the strength of him around her, the warmth of his embrace, his breath on her forehead. He was smiling down at her almost tenderly, and she realized he was actually going to kiss her moments before his lips brushed hers.

Kevin gazed down at her, noting the rose in her cheeks and the slight tremble of her lower lip. She really was a taking little thing. As he had imagined, her curves fit nicely against him. The urge to kiss her was overpowering. He didn't intend to fight it.

She had never been kissed before, not by her suitors during her come-out year, certainly not by those who had sought her out since. She had read a few novels in which the act had been described, and once she had come across a couple together in the moonlit balcony at a ball. Nothing prepared her for Kevin's kiss. It was sweet, it was warm, it was infinitely pleasurable. More, it filled her with a longing to stay this way forever. She trembled at the sheer desire that seemed to be welling up inside her. When he raised his head to gaze down at her, it was all she could do not to pull him to her again.

Kevin had kissed any number of women. He had always found it rather enjoyable, but he was amazed to find that kissing Jenny was something else entirely. Her lips grew more tender the longer he tasted them; just the touch of them made his heart start beating faster. If a kiss could so affect him, what would making love to her be like?

"I think, Miss Welch," he said softly with a gentle smile, "that we have found one area in which we suit admirably."

She stared up at him, too surprised and delighted by the feelings singing through her to move from his embrace.

Kevin could only glory in the feel of her so close. But her silence made him pause. "My dear, if you don't do or say something, I'm very much afraid I shall be forced to kiss you again."

She managed to swallow, her eyes on his face so close to her own. "I . . . I can't seem to move," she whispered.

Her confession was like ice water on his passion. A look of concern crossed his face and he lessened his hold on her. She almost stumbled again as her body betrayed her need for contact.

"Have I shocked you so greatly then?" Kevin murmured, feeling like a cad for pressing his advantage. "Perhaps I should go."

"No! I mean yes. Yes, perhaps you should."

He nodded, moving toward the door with heavy steps. He wasn't sure why he continued to blunder where Jenny Welch was concerned, but this time he knew he had gone too far. He was no better than George Safton, and it shook him to the core.

Jenny sank stunned onto the chair. She felt as if she had gone from fire to ice in a few minutes. She needed time to think through what had just happened. But at the moment, all she could think about was being in his arms again.

Had he been similarly affected? She glanced up at his retreating back and saw how his broad shoulders stooped and his handsome head hung. He thought she was dismissing him. She roused herself.

"Mr. Whattling? Thank you so much . . . for the instruction on boxing. I shall probably have other questions by tomorrow. Do you think you could come again tomorrow afternoon and we could continue our . . . conversation?"

He turned to her and bowed, emotions warring. She was offering him a reprieve. As he gazed at her, it dawned on him that she had been as affected as he had. If she had asked him for the moon just then, he would have done anything to get it for her.

"As you wish, Madam. Until then."

She couldn't have called out to stop him if she had tried.

Fifteen

It took Kevin until the next afternoon to build up the courage to face her again. He couldn't quite understand how he could have been so precipitous. He wasn't exactly known for placing a wager before he had seen his cards. Yet he had seized Jenny as if she were a royal flush and he was a hundred pounds down. He was lucky she hadn't slapped his face!

But his feeling persisted that she had enjoyed the kiss as much as he had. His other experiences told him that the lady's reaction was only to the positive. It boded well for their future together. Suffice it to say, after all was said and done, he was more determined than ever to win her hand. He only hoped he had gauged her feelings correctly.

Although Eugennia was not sure she could admit it, Kevin had judged her feelings exactly. Her reaction to his kiss amazed her. It was some time before she could think clearly. When Miss Tindale arrived with the Egan articles shortly after Kevin had left, Martha found her mistress sitting like a statue, eyes staring off unseeingly. In fact, Martha had to bend down in front of her and look directly in her blank hazel eyes before Eugennia stirred.

"What happened?" Martha demanded. "I knew I

shouldn't leave you alone with that man! What did he do to you?"

Jenny blinked, gazing up at Martha as her abigail straightened. "Oh, hello, Martha. I didn't see you come in. Did you manage to find the Egan articles?"

"Yes, as if you care," Martha snapped, shoving the bundle of articles at her. "And you may as well tell me all. Is Mr. Whattling still welcome in this house?"

Eugennia ran her hands over the top article. "Very welcome. I want you to know, Martha, that if I marry him, I will expect you to stay on. You like children, don't you?"

Martha sank onto the sofa, her skin nearly matching the white satin. "You've accepted him?"

"No, but I am sorely tempted. He kissed me, Martha."

"The bounder," Martha breathed. "What was it like?"

Jenny shivered, closing her eyes and hugging the article to her chest. "It was beyond anything I ever imagined. And I think it affected him as well. Do you think that means he truly cares for me, Martha?"

Miss Tindale's narrow face tightened. "Oh, my dear, I do hope so. I suppose only time will tell. Has Mr. Carstairs gotten back to you with his report yet?"

A chill shot through Eugennia and logic pulled itself firmly back into place. "No, and we should request that he do so." She sighed, rising. "It really is too much to ask to live a fairy tale, isn't it, Martha?"

"I'm afraid so," Martha replied, mirroring her sigh. "Give me back those clippings. I'll return them to Fiching. Then I'll go collect those boxing books and have Stevens return them to the booksellers. Perhaps you can still get your money back."

"Why would I want to do that?" Jenny frowned. "We have a great deal more work to do before I am satisfied we have a comprehensive understanding of the sport."

Martha gaped at her. "But you heard Mr. Whattling. He asked you not to view the sport and you said yourself you could not study it without doing so."

"It is a setback," Jenny agreed. "However, the fact that I cannot play an instrument does not mean I cannot develop an appreciation for music."

"Now you sound like those musicians you sponsor," Martha complained.

Jenny stared at her. "Martha, you are brilliant. Fetch the quill and stationery if you will. I have a letter I'd like you to compose."

Martha rose to comply, but she frowned. "What now?"

Jenny smiled. "It is only to Mr. Carstairs. I wish him to inquire about the price of an item I wish to purchase. I wonder what the going rate is for sponsoring a fighter?"

Kevin was prepared to apologize for his actions when he called the next day. But although Eugennia seemed a bit distracted, she did not mention the incident. Neither did she mention the study of boxing, although he was prepared to discuss that as well. It still amazed him that anyone could get so fascinated with what was written in a book, of all things. When he as much as expressed the thought to Eugennia, she turned to him horrified.

"Do you mean to tell me you don't read?" she gasped, paling.

Kevin gave her his most charming smile, realizing he would have to go carefully on what was obviously a sacred subject to her. "Of course I can read, Miss Welch. I simply find other pursuits more entertaining."

She peered at him as if he had suddenly sprouted a second nose. "Really? How very odd. When was the last time you read a book?"

"An entire book?" he hedged, trying to think. He was

sure he'd better remember accurately, for she'd surely ask him title and text next.

"Yes, an entire book."

He pursed his lips thoughtfully. "I suppose it hasn't been since Eton. I don't actually read much, not even *The Times.*"

She stared at him, eyes wide. "Didn't you even read *The Corsair?*"

He chuckled. "I never particularly liked Byron as a person. I can't imagine I'd like anything he chose to write."

"Then you do have preferences," she persisted. "Do you like poetry, novels, plays, essays, or treatises?"

"Novels, I would say," he replied, though in truth he wasn't sure there was much of a difference. "But nothing overly melodramatic."

"Certainly not," she sniffed.

Miss Tindale sighed. "Oh, I don't know. Fanny Burney wrote such wonderful stories."

Eugennia scowled at her. "Stuff and nonsense. Those works being published anonymously by a 'lady of quality' are far more entertaining. Do you know *Pride and Prejudice,* Mr. Whattling?"

This time he did not hesitate to smile. "I haven't had the pleasure of reading it, Miss Welch, but I can tell you who the author is."

"Really?" she exclaimed. Miss Tindale leaned forward.

Kevin leaned back, enjoying his moment of notoriety. "Indeed. She has even been to see the Regent, who is a most devoted reader, I understand."

"It's not that shocking Caro Lamb, is it?" Miss Tindale guessed. "I don't think I could abide it if it were, although she's always threatening to write something dreadful about society, I hear."

"No, Miss Tindale, not Caro Lamb. She is a Miss Jane Austen, whose father was a clergyman in Hampshire."

Eugennia nodded. "That makes sense. She has an innate understanding of country life that makes her characters seem so real. One would almost think she knew them."

"So I have heard," Kevin nodded.

Eugennia eyed him speculatively. "My reading circle is currently reading *Sense and Sensibility*, Mr. Whattling. Perhaps you would care to join us in discussing its merits and demerits."

Nothing would have pleased him less, but the way she made the offer sounded suspiciously like a challenge, and he was still too much the Corinthian to let any challenge go unaccepted. "That would be delightful, Miss Welch. Just tell me the day and time."

Miss Tindale rolled her eyes and mumbled something as she renewed her attack on the embroidery on her lap.

"It is short notice, I'm afraid," Eugennia told him. "We are discussing it tomorrow at two in the afternoon."

"That should not be a problem," Kevin replied, wondering how long it could take to read a story written by the daughter of a country clergyman.

"Excellent," Jenny nodded. The gleam in her eye told him he had been right to accept the challenge. He only wondered whether he would be able to live up to it.

He met his first obstacle that very afternoon when he found he hadn't enough money in his pocket to purchase the book from a booksellers. And the nearest lending library to his apartments somehow didn't believe his tale of being a long-time patron. Annoyed and shamefaced, he was forced to track down Giles and Nigel at White's and beg for the fee. When he admitted what it was for, they both stared at him.

"A . . . a . . . a book?" Nigel sputtered. "Egads, man, have you gone mad?"

"You aren't actually going to read it, are you, Kev?" Giles pleaded. "You're just going to carry it under one arm, as a sort of prop. She is a bluestocking, after all, Nigel."

"I don't care if she's the heir apparent!" Nigel exclaimed. "No man should have to stoop so low. What does she expect you to read, some female tract against gambling?"

"Nothing so horrendous, old man," Kevin assured him. "Just the latest novel by that Austen woman Prinny was so set on. You may have the book when I'm finished with it if you'd like."

"What do you take me for?" Nigel demanded. "I wouldn't have the thing in my house, no matter what the Regent thinks of it."

"He isn't exactly known for his taste," Giles put in, "if you'll pardon my lack of tact."

"You needn't look so horrified, gentlemen," Kevin repeated. "It is only one book, and it is only to make a good impression. We are agreed that that should still be my plan, are we not?"

Nigel mumbled something, but Giles nodded.

"Very well, then," Kevin continued. "If you can stand to loan me a bit more, I think we shall contrive."

"If you ask me," Nigel grumbled, fishing in the pocket of his waistcoat for a yellow boy, which he tossed to Kevin, "you should be taking a stronger tone with her from the first. You can't wait until after the wedding to let a woman know where you stand on issues—gives them a leg up on a man."

"I think that's a bit strong, Nigel," Giles chided. "Kevin is trying to make a good impression, as he said. I've known many a man to do things while courting he'd never do once he's leg-shackled."

"Well, I suppose," Nigel allowed. "Still, sponsoring boxers and now making Kevin read a book—I don't know ..."

"What?" Kevin interrupted him. "What do you mean, sponsoring boxers?"

Nigel and Giles exchanged glances.

"You didn't know?" Giles asked worriedly.

Kevin was almost afraid to ask, but he had to know the truth. "Didn't know what?"

"It's all about town," Nigel told him. "Her solicitor has been seen at all the boxing establishments. The talk is she's going to choose a fellow and sponsor his fights. He tried to get a name out of Gentleman Jackson and he refused. I naturally assumed you'd been involved somehow."

"No," Kevin replied, jaw tensing. "I wasn't."

Nigel and Giles exchanged glances again.

"Is there more?" Kevin snapped.

Giles jumped. "No, Kev, honestly. It's just that it is rather odd behavior. I mean, what lady involves herself with pugilists, of all things?"

"I certainly hope, Giles," Kevin replied, watching his friend shrink under his steely gaze, "that you are not implying that Miss Welch is anything less than a lady?"

"No, no," Giles gasped. "Never! Nigel, tell him!"

"Cut line, Kevin," Nigel growled. "If you mean to take on everyone who implies Miss Welch has no business with boxers, you'll have to fight every gossip in town."

"As bad as that," Kevin frowned.

"Afraid so, old man," Nigel told him.

"I don't know where you stand in your pursuit of the lady," Giles put in. "But you may want to have a word with her on her behavior, for her own good, you know."

"I have had a word with her, Giles," Kevin replied, rising. "Several words to be exact. But I have a feeling it will take a great deal more to dissuade Eugennia Welch from her studies."

Sixteen

He arrived precisely at two in the afternoon on the following day, book tucked under his arm. His navy coat and trousers were as immaculate as ever, and none of the three ladies or two gentlemen he was introduced to noticed the dark circles under his eyes from staying up all night reading. They also failed to notice that he was sweating.

"So good of you to join us, Mr. Whattling," a white-haired woman with double chins nodded as Eugennia introduced her as Mrs. Bryce-Turner. "We so seldom get new blood these days."

"And what exactly is wrong with old blood, I'd like to know?" Lord Davies, an equally elderly gentleman demanded. He thumped his attendant cane on the floor so hard that the vase on the nearby credenza rattled.

"I don't think Mrs. Bryce-Turner was maligning us, Lord Davies," the other gentleman, a younger man with sandy blond hair and a weak chin murmured. "I believe she was referring to the pleasant addition of another point of view, by your leave, of course, Mrs. B."

She nodded graciously at him.

"An excellent encapsulation, Mr. Witherspoon," agreed the dark-haired young lady who alone besides Eugennia could make any claim to beauty. She turned expressive eyes an exotic shade of light green on him, and he tried not to flinch from the direct gaze. "Let us hope Mr. Whattling has come prepared to discuss the book in question."

"Why ever would he not, Miss St. John?" Miss Tindale put in, offering Kevin an innocent smile that he could not return. Eugennia piped up, sitting beside him on the sofa. "I have come to appreciate the fact that Mr. Whattling is quite talented in many areas. I'm sure he will acquit himself well."

The look from those hazel eyes did something to the center of his being, and he suddenly found he was capable of climbing mountains. "I can only say, Miss Welch," he murmured, "that I perform in accordance with my inspiration."

She blushed prettily.

Susan St. John snapped open the book. "Well said. And did you find the hero of this piece as well spoken, Mr. Whattling?"

"If by the hero, you mean the character of Edward, Miss St. John," Kevin replied, leaning back against the sofa, "no, I did not."

"I take it you didn't like him," Mrs. Bryce-Turner put in.

"It wasn't so much that I didn't like him, Madam. He was a well-developed character, I thought. I simply would not approach life as he chose to do. In fact, I would not approach life like any of the gentlemen in this book."

"Really, sir," Lord Davies protested. "Did you not find Colonel Brandon the least heroic? Now, there was a gentleman."

"A gentleman who allowed his first love to be led astray and then refused to acknowledge his love for Miss Marianne until she was at death's door." Kevin shook his head. "I hope I am never so foolish. Life is entirely too short."

"I suppose you agree with the character of Willoughby,

then," Susan St. John put in, narrowing her exquisite eyes even as she mirrored Eugennia's thought from the other day. "Live life and never mind the consequences."

He looked down at his hands as they gripped the closed book. As he forced himself to release it on his lap, Eugennia could see dents in the fine-tooled leather cover where his fingers had rested. "I once thought that way. It is a dangerous sport, more suited to the very young, I believe. The true man grows quickly beyond that. Live life, yes, but do not do so in a way that inhibits another's ability to live."

"Well said, sir, well said," Lord Davies exclaimed, thumping his cane again. Mr. Witherspoon regarded him with worshipful eyes. Mrs. Bryce-Turner beamed. Even Miss Tindale grimaced in approval. Miss St. John nodded, leaning back against her chair as if satisfied. It was all Eugennia could do not to crow her delight.

It was a wonderful discussion, and all the members of her circle insisted that Kevin be included in the next reading. As she saw them out one by one, they let her know their personal approval as well.

"Quite kind on the eyes, that one," Mrs. Bryce-Turner whispered behind her glove as she shrugged into her fur-trimmed pelisse. "If he offers, accept. If he doesn't, would you mind if I introduced him to my niece?"

"Capital fellow," Lord Davies proclaimed, after bowing over her hand. "Welcome addition to the group, and to the family, eh, my dear?"

"A regular top-o'-the-trees Corinthian," Mr. Witherspoon confided, adjusting his top hat in the entryway mirror. "And bookish, too. Such a find!"

"He's too perfect," Susan St. John told her, hugging her good day. "I don't know whether to envy you or worry for you. Be careful, dearest. This one could steal your heart."

Eugennia could only smile politely as Susan left. She turned to find Kevin eyeing her.

"Am I to take it that my performance lived up to your expectations, Miss Welch?" he asked.

She frowned. "Twice now you have called it a performance, sir. I wonder, are you performing?"

"I am wounded," he professed, but the twinkle in his indigo eyes belied his serious tone. "I'll have you know I read every word on every page of this book, Miss Welch, no mean feat, let me assure you."

"Yes," she nodded, "but did you enjoy it?"

He looked thoughtful. "Yes, but not in the way I would have suspected. It was an interesting look at our society. It certainly made me think."

She beamed at him. "That is precisely what good literature is supposed to do, Mr. Whattling. I'm very glad you enjoyed Miss Austen's book. Dare I hope you will take us up on our offer to join the next discussion?"

He cocked his head. "What are we reading?"

"Nothing vile," she promised with a laugh. "Susan would like to continue reading Miss Austen's books. The next is *Pride and Prejudice.*"

"That could be interesting," he nodded. "Very well. When will this discussion take place?"

"Two weeks from today," she told him.

"Ah, that is a shame. I hope to be otherwise engaged at that time."

She fought not to look disappointed. "Oh? You have something scheduled so far in advance?"

He smiled at her. "I understand it is necessary to plan at least a little ahead for one's wedding, Miss Welch."

She could feel her face burning in a blush and had to look away. "I do not believe we have decided we have anything to plan, sir."

"Miss Welch," he murmured, taking her hand. "You cannot keep me dangling forever, you know. While I would gladly wait an eternity for your answer, my creditors, alas, are not so smitten. I have been courting you rather assiduously for nearly a fortnight now. Can you say you feel nothing for me?"

She knew she could say nothing of the kind. His solicitous attention, his flirtatious conversation, his brilliant literary insights, and his amazing kiss stirred her heart as no one had ever done. She would have loved to have accepted his offer, but she still could not credit that it was not her fortune that motivated him. Would he still be the wonderful man he seemed once he knew he had the money? Or was he simply more adept at play-acting than George Safton? Would she find herself married to some horrible creature? If only there were some way to be sure. She raised her head to tell him her fears, but one look in those deep blue eyes sealed her lips. She simply wasn't sure she wanted to know the answer.

Kevin smiled. Did she know how transparent her thoughts were? He had all but won. A few more visits and she would accept him. "You do not have to answer that," he told her.

She started to relax.

"At least, not now," he grinned. "Until tomorrow, Miss Welch." He bowed over her hand and pressed a kiss on her wrist. Jenny shivered despite herself.

Fiching recovered himself sufficiently to whisk open the door for him. Kevin nearly collided with a liveried footman. Fiching took the proffered cards and waved the man off. Recognizing the telltale handwriting, Kevin smiled.

"If I am not mistaken," he said with a tip of his hat to Eugennia, "those are your promised vouchers for Almack's."

Eugennia refused to so much as touch them as Fiching held them out to her hopefully. "Yes, they look very like the last one that came. I'll have Miss Tindale express my gratitude again, but I still cannot accept."

Kevin stepped back into the entry hall, frowning. "You turned Countess Lieven down? My God, woman, are you bent on suicide?"

Eugennia tossed her head with far more bravery than she felt. "I told you, I have no interest in going to Almack's."

"Why ever not?" Kevin's frown deepened. "Isn't that the pinnacle to which all London ladies aspire?"

"Perhaps some London ladies with nothing more interesting to do with their time than primp before their looking glasses," Eugennia replied scornfully. "They only want me there because I'm an oddity. I have no interest in being the evening's entertainment, I assure you."

He took her hand again and looked down at her, so proud and so fearful of their scorn. "I would never let them use you so."

"You have a high regard for your own abilities, Mr. Whattling."

He grinned. "Yes, Miss Welch, I do."

She fought to answer the grin. "I thank you for your concern. But I'm not going to Almack's, so you may save your breath."

"I cannot believe you are truly afraid of them," he persisted. "And I know you are perfectly able to carry a conversation. Your natural curiosity has to have been piqued. What exactly is it about Almack's that you think will be so bad that you refuse to go?"

She scowled at him for several seconds, then threw up her hands. "Oh, very well, if you must know. I can't dance."

Kevin raised an eyebrow. "I beg your pardon?"

"I can't dance. And they will all expect it of me, especially if I show up on your arm. Oh, I can manage a country dance or two, but nothing beyond it. I will stand there, the epitome of the spinster, exactly the prudish bluestocking they expect me to be, and I cannot bear it!" She could feel the tears welling and turned away from him to hide it.

"Miss Welch," he murmured, stepping closer. He bent his head to her ear. "Jenny, please don't distress yourself. If that is all that is stopping you, let me help. I would be delighted to teach you to dance."

She sniffed, brushing him away from her hair with a movement of her hand. "Why would I want you to do that?"

"Because it would be educational, my dear," he replied, and she could tell he was trying to lighten her mood. "And I do believe that is one area in which you excel, is it not?"

That won a reluctant smile. "You know very well it is."

"Excellent. Then I suggest we start tomorrow and continue until next Wednesday, when it will be my pleasure to escort you to Almack's."

George Safton traced figures on the mahogany table with the base of the crystal wine goblet. Anyone watching him would have thought him an idiot or drunk to be so easily amused. George was neither. He was highly frustrated, and this simple act was all he could manage without betraying himself.

Wagers were being placed. Several had already been recorded in the famed betting book at White's. Kevin Whattling was moments away from becoming engaged to Eugennia Welch. There didn't seem to be a thing George could do to stop it.

The matter was becoming urgent. Twice in the last week he had attempted to arrange fights, but no one was willing to put up the purse. In fact, he hadn't found many willing to play cards or interest themselves in his newest thoroughbred either. If he didn't find a willing body soon, his pockets would be as empty as Kevin Whattling's.

He was still sure that discrediting Kevin was the best approach, but each attempt to involve himself in Whattling's or Miss Welch's affairs had been thwarted. Whattling hadn't taken her out in public for days (not that he blamed Kevin in that regard), he hadn't been able to catch them in the park even though it seemed he haunted its lanes, and she was avoiding Curzon Street altogether. Cloistered as they were, he had no opportunity to observe them and hence none to make his mark.

The one small bit of information he had heard was that Miss Welch had taken a sudden interest in boxers. He would have loved to have taken her money for one of his pugilists, but he didn't think even going through her solicitor would hide his involvement, and she was hardly likely to put money into anything connected with George. So far, he had not been able to think of a way around the difficulties. He just needed to give it more thought.

It was ironic, but perhaps the very sport that had made him suspect would serve to clear his name. He would simply have to wait and see.

Seventeen

Unfortunately, Kevin proved to be singularly useless as a dance master. He knew the dances well enough, but Eugennia found it impossible to remember the steps when she never knew when the touch of his hand would send tremors through her. She simply could not concentrate with him so near. By the end of the first hour, she had completely lost patience.

"You are trying too hard," Kevin told her when she stepped on his boot for the third time. As she wasn't heavy and his boots were sturdy Hessians, the accidents didn't bother him. But he could tell they bothered her greatly. Poor bluestocking, she wasn't used to having difficulty learning a new subject.

"I don't know how not to try hard," Eugennia maintained heatedly. "Let me alone for a moment."

Miss Tindale obligingly kept playing at the polished pianoforte in the corner of Eugennia's music room, and Kevin stepped back from Eugennia's side, carefully avoiding the music stands propped nearby. Truth be told, the room was not conducive to such practices, but they needed music and it held the piano. Like many of the other rooms he had observed in Eugennia's house, it was done in shades of blue and rose and saffron, making it calming and sunny even though it held only two small windows looking on the rear yard of the house. Also like many rooms, it seemed to him to hold a few more pieces of furniture than it needed, boasting the piano, three rows of lute-backed chairs, two decorative tables, and the music stands. Although the chairs had been pushed into the farthest corner and the stands against the wall, it didn't leave much room to dance. Still, he couldn't exactly demand another room.

Jenny frowned as she walked through the last steps of the dance they had been practicing. Her puce silk rustled with her movements. Left then right, no right then left. Turn. Curtsey. Rise. She stopped, and the frown increased.

"Go on," Kevin urged her encouragingly. "You were doing splendidly."

Jenny shook her head. "No, I just crashed into the second couple. I believe it was the gentleman."

Kevin grinned at her. "He will no doubt find it a delightful experience, and you will be besieged by other offers to dance. Brazen it out, and keep going."

Jenny nodded, returning to the figure again. She took three more steps and threw up her hands. "Blast!"

Miss Tindale stopped playing with a gasp.

"Sorry, Martha," she apologized, blushing. "Now I've run into the lady. And don't you dare say she will take it as a compliment, Mr. Whattling, or I shall laugh in your face!"

"Better to laugh than to cry," Kevin countered, returning to her side. "Or to curse, shall we say. I think I shall play stern teacher and tell you that we should stop for today. It was never my intention to upset you."

"I upset myself," Eugennia declared, shaking her head in vexation. "You have been more than patient. I agree— let's give this up as a lost cause."

"Thank goodness," Miss Tindale sighed, wringing her

frail hands. "I don't think I could have played much longer anyway."

Kevin eyed Jenny's downcast head. "Only for today, now. I refuse to give up on you."

"Why ever not?" Eugennia snapped. "I tried to explain to you that I cannot dance. Nothing you can do in two days' time is going to change that."

"Have you so little faith in me?" Kevin replied, catching her hand and pressing it. "Or so little faith in yourself? What you need is a change of scene. What say we go for a drive?"

"I suppose you brought the curricle," Martha sniffed before Jenny could answer.

Kevin grinned at her, offering a bow. "Regretfully true, Miss Tindale. But I will bring her back unharmed. I promise."

Martha sniffed again.

Driving somehow did not sound any more pleasant to Jenny than what they had been doing, but she found she could not gainsay him. A moment's analysis told her why, and she went to summon Fiching for her pelisse and bonnet so that she could hide her blush. It was patently obvious that what she really wanted was an excuse to be alone with Kevin so that he might have an opportunity to kiss her again. That wasn't likely to happen in Hyde Park, but she couldn't help but feel her spirits rise as Kevin helped her into the white curricle and they set out.

It was another balmy spring day, as if they were being rewarded for their choice of pastime. He and Eugennia drove slowly through the park, stopping frequently to converse with acquaintances. The people they met were pleasant, and Eugennia found the drive less taxing than she had expected. It gave her the feeling that she might master this social nonsense after all. They had completed the circuit and were heading back toward the exit on Park Lane, when a hail from behind made Kevin slow the horses once more. "Can you stand another effusive greeting?" he asked Eugennia with a wink.

She smiled at him. "As long as you keep the conversation off the weather, your horses, or your cravat."

He grinned back at her. "I promise, even if I have to be rude about it." He pulled the horses to a stop and glanced back over his shoulder at the approaching rider. That look was all it took for him to face forward and take out the whip.

"Mr. Whattling?" Eugennia asked, gripping the side-board as the horses jerked forward.

"It's Safton," Kevin murmured, steering around a slow-moving landau with difficulty. "Hang on. I'll try to lose him."

Eugennia nodded, throat constricting. She reminded herself sternly that they were in a public park; the man could hardly accost them there. Yet somehow, she could not convince herself of their safety. As they careened around the landau, a knot of riders appeared in front of them. Horses reared, and ladies cried out. With a muffled curse, Kevin slowed the horses once more.

Safton drew abreast on Eugennia's side. In his red riding coat and black breeches, he should have looked like the dashing Corinthian he tried to pretend to be. But under the fashionable shock of untidy black hair, the dark eyes glittered with triumphant menace.

"Kevin Whattling!" he declared in ringing tones. "Pull up, man. We must talk."

"Another time, Safton," Kevin bit off. "As you can see, I am otherwise engaged."

Eugennia kept her eyes resolutely on the path ahead, determined not to so much as acknowledge the man's existence. She could only hope that Safton would take the obvious hint and leave them alone.

George wasn't about to let them go. This was the opportunity he had been waiting for. All he had to do was play his cards right, and Whattling would tumble into his trap. And the best card he could play was Eugennia Welch herself.

"Petticoat be hanged," George snapped. "You've been avoiding me for weeks. You still owe me over two thousand, and I want to know when I'll see it."

Kevin's jaw was tense. "Not now, George."

"Damnation, Whattling, don't you take that tone with me. You're the one who should be begging for favors. Ah, but then you are, aren't you? How does it feel to earn your money at the lady's expense?"

Eugennia gave up her attempt at ignoring the creature. She favored him with her coldest glare. "That is quite enough, Mr. Safton. I think Mr. Whattling has made it perfectly clear that your presence isn't wanted."

She had sand—Safton would give her that. But he wasn't about to give up. "Well of course my presence isn't wanted. You have the gentleman you've purchased. Tell me, my dear, do you pay him by the mile or for services rendered?"

Eugennia felt herself paling. She vainly struggled to find something to say to put the odious fellow in his place.

"That's enough, George," Kevin said quietly. She would have had to have been deaf not to hear the anger in his voice. His blue eyes were chips of ice, and his hands gripped the reins so hard he threatened to snap the sturdy leather. "Take yourself off now. I'll meet you at Watier's later."

"Very well, Whattling," George purred, satisfied that he had at least won a small victory. But he couldn't help capping his triumph with one last parting shot. "Miss Welch, your servant. If young Whattling proves less than satisfactory, you may always call on me. A woman willing to pay for favors ought to get her money's worth."

"Damnation!" Kevin yanked the reins so hard that one of Nigel's whites reared in confusion. The horse's movement effectively blocked Safton's escape. As Eugennia gasped, Kevin practically leapt over her to reach the ground at Safton's side.

"You will apologize to the lady at once, Safton," he growled through clenched teeth, "or by God I'll rip that smile off your face at last."

Safton controlled his black with difficulty, amazed that he had actually scored so effectively. "Don't be a fool, Whattling. Dueling's against the law. You ought to remember that."

Kevin smiled up at him, and there was nothing of his usual warmth. It chilled Eugennia to the bone to see it, and she thought she saw Safton swallow. "Oh, I don't want to shoot you, George. It would give me far greater satisfaction to beat you to death with my bare hands."

A light sprang to Safton's dark eyes. This was better than he had ever planned. "A fight? You're on. Jackson's, Friday, three in the afternoon. I'll make the arrangements." He jerked his horse around, gave it the boot, and raced through the crush of carriages, cries of alarm and surprise echoing in his wake.

Kevin stood impotently watching him, seething. He found he couldn't face Eugennia and strode around the carriage instead to regain his seat.

Eugennia saw him take up the reins and start the horses forward once more. The veneer of the Corinthian was gone. So was Hamlet and Puck and her pharaoh. In their place was a man who had just confronted his worst enemy and the act had left him shaken but determined. Safton was a beast. But his insult to her did not warrant such a vehement response from Kevin. Something else was obviously driving him.

"You don't have to go through with that," she told him as the carriage at last reached the exit.

"On the contrary, Miss Welch," he replied calmly as if nothing untoward had happened. "Nothing would give me more pleasure."

"I believe that's what you said about courting me, sir."

His face was still pale and shuttered as he set the horses at a smart clip down Park Lane. "This has nothing to do with you, Jenny. Safton has been a thorn in my side for months. It's time I excised it."

She wanted to take pleasure in the fact that he had used her pet name, but under the circumstances, she found it difficult. "I see. Then I am right in thinking that it truly didn't matter to you that he insulted me just now."

Kevin started. In truth, he had jumped in because Safton dared to insult her, on top of all the other things the miscreant had done. "It matters a great deal," Kevin told her quietly. "You might say it was the catalyst that made me see I must take him on directly. George Safton is a monster. I finally understand why some call him The Snake. I shall be only too pleased to shove that snake back under his rock."

Eugennia had a sudden image of a large cobra striking back at Kevin. She shuddered and tried again. "I agree that he is odious, but he spoke no more than the truth in the eyes of the ton. For all that I enjoy your company, Mr. Whattling, you have never made any pretense as to what brought you to my door. Can you honestly say you'd be driving me through Hyde Park today if it wasn't for my fortune?"

He turned to her, blue eyes blazing. "Yes. If I didn't

have these accursed debts and we had met under other circumstances, I'd still be driving you through Hyde Park today and I'd still be courting you every day until you agree to my suit. I happen to be in love with you, Madam."

Jenny stared at him, color draining. His words were words she'd dreamed of hearing him say, but his anger belied them. "I . . . I cannot have heard you correctly."

"Why?" he demanded, too frustrated to notice her response to his precipitous announcement. "Because Corinthians aren't supposed to have feelings? Neither are bluestockings, or so I'd heard. I'll reserve the right to fall in love when I so choose, thank you very much. Despite George Safton's poisonous tongue, my love doesn't come with a price on it."

"I see," Jenny replied quietly, overcome. "It's only your honor you wished me to purchase."

"That is quite enough," Kevin snapped. "I do not understand why you insist on seeing yourself as the beggar in this situation. I'm the one who's in debt, I'm the one begging for favors. There is no shame on you. I don't care what anyone may tell you. You are perfectly capable of forming your own opinions, my girl. Instead of seeing your intellect as a handicap, perhaps you should begin to use it to your advantage."

"But it is precisely my intellect that tells me you cannot be courting me because you love me. I am scarcely a renowned beauty, you know that I cannot converse well in society, and we both know what an abysmal dancer I am. How can you possibly love me?"

"Do you think those are the only things that count? What about spirit, Madam, patience, generosity? How many women do you know who would put up with a companion as quarrelsome as Miss Tindale? How many women would struggle to learn all they can of the world around them?"

Jenny looked away from him as tears threatened. "Those things are far more important, I agree. I simply never met a gentleman who thought so."

"Well, you've met one now." He glanced over at her and all his anger melted. Tears trickled down her broad cheeks, her little nose was turning red, and her lower lip trembled pathetically. She really was the most taking little thing.

"It's all right, Jenny," he murmured, reaching out to squeeze her hand beside him on the carriage seat. "I'm sorry I was so cross. You are quite right that this encounter with Safton has upset me more than I care to admit. I'll take you home. And I promise to be a much more patient teacher tomorrow."

Eighteen

Eugennia could barely say goodbye when Kevin walked her to her door. He tried to be his usual charming self, but all she could manage at his sallies was a watery smile. She let Fiching take her pelisse gratefully, in anticipation of retreating to her room for some time alone to try to understand her own feelings. Her handsome prince had just declared his love for her, although in a rather uncharming manner, especially for him. She wasn't sure whether to laugh or continue crying. She was therefore quite dismayed to find that she had a visitor.

"He says he wanted to thank you personally for your donation to his efforts to raise money for the British prisoners still in France. Miss Tindale has been entertaining him for perhaps a quarter hour." He nudged her toward the sitting room door with his elbow. "We don't get many chances to meet the likes of Gentleman Jackson, Miss Jenny. Don't you think you could go in and see him, at least for a short time?"

Jenny sighed. It was hardly Mr. Jackson's fault that she was so preoccupied. Besides, given the upcoming fight between Kevin and Mr. Safton, she was already forming questions, questions which a noted expert on the ring could answer.

"Very well, Fiching," she nodded, allowing him to open the door for her.

Jackson rose as she entered. She wasn't sure what she had been expecting after hearing and reading so much about him, perhaps an older version of Kevin. Gentleman Jackson stood a little shorter than Kevin. For all that the ex-fighter was approaching fifty, the muscular build that had won him such fame and made him the favorite of painters and sculptors was still evident in the red jacket and tight black trousers he wore. However, aside from his height and build, there was little other resemblance. John Jackson's shock of gray hair did not hide the fact that his forehead sloped and his ears stuck straight out from the side of his head. His high cheekbones were eclipsed by a rather coarse nose and mouth. Most prominent of all, however, were a pair of piercing eyes that made her want to stand a little straighter.

"Oh, Eugennia, how nice," Miss Tindale clarioned from her spot on the sofa. "May I introduce Mr. John Jackson of London. Mr. Jackson, Miss Eugennia Welch."

He stepped forward and bowed over her hand. "Miss Welch, a pleasure. I'm sorry for the intrusion, but I had to thank you for your generous donation."

She could understand how he'd earned the appellation of Gentleman with his courtly manner. Jenny nodded in acknowledgment of his thanks, going to sit beside Martha on the sofa. Jackson resumed his seat on the nearest chair.

"You are quite welcome, Mr. Jackson," she told him. "I have to admit, however, that it was a rather calculating gift."

He raised an eyebrow. "Oh, how so?"

"You may have heard that I have a certain reputation as a bluestocking," she replied. "I am currently studying the art of boxing. I understand you refused to talk to my solicitor Mr. Carstairs when he appeared at your Pugilistic Club, so I thought perhaps a large gift might get you to come here to me."

"Not that she doesn't care about the prisoners of war," Miss Tindale put in. "We are both quite concerned about them."

"As are we all," Jackson nodded. He eyed Jenny appraisingly, and she once again caught herself straightening under the sharp gaze. "I apologize for not hearing your solicitor out. I'm afraid we've had a number of requests to sponsor fighters, and I'm very careful with whom I align my students."

"Understandable," Jenny replied. "But I wanted to assure you that I am only interested in pursuing studies. Whether the fighter wins or looses, whether he fights once or half a dozen times, is immaterial to me."

Jackson looked thoughtful. "So you wish to study boxing, Miss Welch. You aren't actually thinking of fighting yourself, are you?"

"Good heavens, no!" Martha declared adamantly.

Jenny frowned her into silence. "I must admit I seldom enjoy the luxury of putting into practice what I study, Mr. Jackson. People are scandalized enough that I study it. I shudder to think what they would do if I actually lived it."

He nodded wisely. "Very sensible. Of course, I must tell you that there are women boxers here in London. They have regular practices and bouts, just as the men do."

"Really?" Martha breathed. "Anyone we might know?"

"Most assuredly not, Miss Tindale," Jackson told her quellingly. However, Eugennia got the impression he was merely trying to forestall gossip rather than censuring the women pugilists. "I only mention them to show that there are a number of ways for women to participate in the sport. However, if it is only a matter of curiosity, you needn't go so far as to sponsor a fighter, Miss Welch. I'd be happy to answer any questions you might have."

She had had dozens of questions concerning the sport, but none of them seemed important at the moment. There was only one thing on her mind. "How can I get to see a fight?"

"If there is an issue of a lady's reputation as you indicated," he frowned, "I wouldn't imagine you'd be any less ostracized for viewing a fight as sponsoring a fighter or taking up the sport yourself."

"Of course she'd be ostracized," Martha declared. She turned to her mistress with a scowl. "I thought you had given up on that idea, Eugennia. Mr. Whattling and I have both told you this isn't wise."

"And I agreed with you," Jenny acknowledged impatiently, "until Mr. Whattling challenged Mr. Safton to a fight."

Jackson's frown deepened. "Kevin Whattling is fighting George Safton? Are you certain?"

"Certain," Jenny told him. "Mr. Safton will be coming to you to make the arrangements. He wants to do it this coming Friday."

"I would be quite tempted to refuse," Jackson confided. "Safton has avoided having his fights at my establishment because he knows I won't countenance his tricks."

Now Eugennia frowned. "Safton has had other fights?"

"Mr. Safton rarely enters the ring himself. He's usually the one selecting the fighters and holding the purse. He also takes a healthy share of the money if the rumors are true. Then there was that business with Robbie Greene."

Eugennia started. "What business?"

Jackson eyed her again. "I think perhaps you'd better ask Mr. Whattling that question. Suffice it to say that Mr. Safton has an unsavory reputation when it comes to arranging fights. However, I will most likely allow them to hold the fight at my rooms or Five Courts, as I'd be afraid Mr. Whattling might not get a fair fight if Mr. Safton were left to his own devices."

"What do you mean?" Eugennia asked sharply as Miss Tindale gazed at him wide-eyed. "How can a fight be unfair?"

"In any number of ways," Jackson replied. "For all it can be a punishing sport, there are rules. When people abide by the rules, a fight will be fought fairly."

"And several gentlemen have been trying to make it safer, as we've read," Miss Tindale remarked. "Breaks between rounds, umpires, that sort of thing."

"That's right," Jackson nodded. "But despite these advances, there are still ways to ensure your opponent looses. I've seen fights where poison was put in a man's water bottle or the other fighter ignored the umpires and broke a man's back while he was down. Are you all right, Miss Welch?"

Eugennia barely managed a nod. She knew she must look as sick as she felt, for Martha was staring at her, concerned as well.

"Are you saying," Jenny managed to rasp out, "that Mr. Whattling might be hurt in this fight?"

"I'm saying," Jackson replied firmly, "that Mr. Whattling could be killed."

Miss Tindale gasped. Eugennia rose to her feet. Jackson was forced to do likewise.

"Then we must stop it," she told him. "What can be done?"

Jackson shook his head. "I doubt there's anything we can do, Miss Welch. Even if you could somehow convince the two gentlemen to settle their differences in another manner, they'll be honor-bound to go through with the fight, because an event of this nature will already be the talk of London."

"Then the magistrates will hear of it," Martha sniffed, stabbing at her embroidery. "They will surely stop it."

Jackson chuckled wryly. "If I know Mr. Safton, he's already paid off anyone who might have made a protest. And Mr. Whattling is rather popular. The magistrates will be only too delighted to place wagers along with everyone else. It wouldn't surprise me if they didn't turn out to watch the match."

"Is there nothing we can do to ensure Mr. Whattling's safety?" Eugennia pressed, stomach churning.

Jackson eyed her. "Possibly. There may be a way you can help, Miss Welch. But it will involve some risk on your part."

"Anything," Eugennia agreed.

Miss Tindale started to protest, but the look on Jenny's face silenced her.

Jackson glanced between the two of them, then motioned Jenny back to her seat, returning to his seat himself. He leaned forward conspiratorially. Even Martha was forced to pay attention.

"There are two gentlemen who feel the way I do about Mr. Safton," he explained. "There are also any number of others who he has wronged. It would be my pleasure to help them bring him to justice. But if we are to get him to show his true colors, we must make it worth his while. I know I cautioned you against getting actively involved in boxing, Miss Welch, but if you'd be willing to put up a purse for this event, I think the results would be well worth the price."

"What were you thinking?" Nigel demanded when Kevin answered his knock that evening.

Kevin grimaced, moving aside to let him and Giles enter. "I take it you heard about my fight with Safton."

"It's the talk of the town," Giles confirmed. "You must have had great provocation, Kevin."

Kevin ran his hand back through his hair. "It seemed so at the time."

"Ah, but now I'll wager you're regretting it," Nigel declared.

Kevin shook his head. "Surprisingly no, gentlemen. I probably should have done this long ago."

"You'll get no argument from me that Safton deserves it," Nigel growled, pacing. "But you know this won't be a fair fight. He'll find some way to rig it in his favor."

"Possibly," Kevin allowed. "But this isn't a professional match like the one he arranged for Robbie. I know where and when it will be held and I know my opponent. I don't think Robbie knew he was fighting the Giant until the beast climbed into the ring. And he hardly expected that filthy tavern at the back of beyond as the stage. I think I've stacked the odds well on my side. What can Safton do at Gentleman Jackson's?"

"Very little, I would guess," Giles put in. "Still, it seems a shame to chance it. I suppose there's no way you can get out of it?"

"None that leaves my honor in tact," Kevin replied. "I issued the challenge when he insulted Miss Welch."

Nigel threw up his hands. "I knew that woman was involved! Did you have to impress her this much?"

Kevin smiled. "I have to admit, Nigel, that that was a small part of it. However, you know my feelings for Safton. This meeting was inevitable. Would you rather it was pistols at dawn?"

"Only if I could be sure Safton was the loser," Nigel muttered.

Kevin's smile deepened. "You can be sure of that in this case, Nigel. I've seen him fight."

"So have I," Giles put in. "His reach is longer than yours, Kevin. And he has a punishing right."

Kevin shrugged. "So be it. Thank you for your assessment, Giles. I'll try to remember it. I hope I can count on both of you for this event."

"You don't have to ask," Nigel growled. "We wouldn't allow you to do it alone."

"What can we do?" Giles chimed in.

"Will you serve as my knee and bottlemen?"

They nodded solemnly in unison.

Kevin clapped them both on the shoulders. "Capital! Then all we need do is visit the Gentleman tomorrow and arrange practice times."

"You might as well ask Miss Welch," Nigel replied with a humph. "The story is that he was up to her home this afternoon, shortly after your unfortunate meeting with Safton."

Kevin frowned. "But why? Surely she isn't still set on this course of study."

"Study!" Nigel sneered. "Is that what she calls it? If you ask me, this woman has been nothing but trouble. I hope you'll give up on this plan of yours now."

"Why, Nigel? The lady can hardly be blamed for creating friction between Safton and me. Besides, I find myself anticipating the end of this adventure. I hope you will shortly be wishing me happiness."

Giles beamed and Nigel rolled his eyes. "She's going to accept you?"

"I have high hopes," Kevin grinned. "And you may as well know the whole of it. I'd marry her even if she were penniless. I appear to have fallen in love with her, gentlemen."

Nigel gaped. Giles clapped Kevin on the shoulder.

"Splendid news, Kevin!" he crowed. "It goes without saying that the lady will reciprocate. This is marvelous!"

"Yes, well, congratulations," Nigel managed. "Now we only have to see that you live to see your wedding day."

Nineteen

The next afternoon found Eugennia staring out the sitting room windows, impatient for Kevin's arrival. She had spent a restless night wondering whether Mr. Jackson's plan would be effective. There was no doubt in her mind that Kevin was infinitely more talented and intelligent than the odious Mr. Safton, but until Gentleman Jackson had pointed out the potential for foul play, she had never truly considered that Kevin might not win. Worse, that Kevin might actually be hurt! She refused to think about the chance that he might be killed. Life without any chance of seeing him again was simply too empty.

She might as well admit it aloud, she realized. She had fallen in love with the man Kevin Whattling portrayed. To do herself justice, she knew it was a logical choice. He was everything she had ever thought a man should be—intelligent, witty, handsome, caring, gentle. What woman would have not fallen in love with such a paragon? But loving him or no, she couldn't watch him be hurt. The prize money seemed like a far cry from stopping the fight. She needed to construct an argument that would keep Kevin from setting foot in the ring.

She was so agitated that she could barely contain herself while Fiching announced Kevin's arrival. Kevin noticed the change in her immediately. Her round face was as white as the collar of her lilac lustring gown, dark circles ringed her expressive eyes, and her movements were quick and tremulous. He did not need to notice that Miss Tindale was absent to realize that Eugennia wanted to talk to him alone about a matter of some urgency.

"What's happened?" he asked, taking her hands as Fiching went to stand outside the open door.

Once more her flawless arguments failed her. "You must call off this fight," she burst out. Her hands in his shook. "I cannot bear the thought that you might be hurt."

"Why, Eugennia," he murmured, touched by her concern. He let go of her hands and brushed a stray silken hair away from her face. "Do not worry, my dear. Safton will finally get his comeuppance."

She jerked away from his touch. "I don't care about George Safton! I do care about you! Gentleman Jackson says you might be killed!"

So the rumors were true; she had been seeing the Gentleman, and on close terms if her confession was any indication. He smothered a sudden absurd burst of jealousy. "Much as I value the Gentleman's opinion, he is mistaken in this case."

"Can you be so confident of victory?" Eugennia frowned, unwilling to be convinced too easily.

"I can be confident of beating George Safton to a bloody pulp."

Even though he grinned as he said it, the thought chilled Eugennia to the core. She wrung her hands. "I wish I'd never started this study of boxing!"

"That would hardly change this fight," Kevin reminded her, watching her with concern.

"But why must you fight?" she demanded. "He insulted me, not you. And I assure you I could care less what George Safton thinks of me."

Kevin attempted to capture her hands again, but she turned from him so quickly that he only touched air. "Safton and I have other differences that have nothing to do with you," he assured her.

"Surely there is another way to solve those differences," Eugennia protested.

Kevin gave up watching her and grabbed a hand. "I have tried, believe me. Let it go, Jenny. It will all turn out in the end, I promise. We have more important matters to discuss."

"What could possibly be more important than your life?" she demanded.

He grinned. "Your debut at Almack's, of course."

She rolled her eyes, exasperated. "Will you never believe me? That is inconsequential under the circumstances!"

"On the contrary. Your attendance with me is now critical. Would you have me branded a coward?"

It was an overstatement, he knew, but he was pleased to see her logical mind seize on the issue. Anything was worth a try to get her off this subject of the fight.

"Who would dare utter such a ridiculous statement, and what has that to do with my attendance at Almack's?" she frowned.

"It is well known I am courting you. As you observed yourself earlier, they will expect you to show up on my arm. If we do not show up, what will they think?"

That was an easy answer. She had feared it all along. "They will think I am too much the bluestocking to appreciate the honor of their company."

He shook his head. "Not necessarily. Given the advent of this fight, they are more likely to think I am too craven to face them."

"Never!" she scowled.

"Then we are agreed we must attend together?"

She sighed. "I still cannot completely agree to your reasoning, but I concede that you know society's whims far better than I do. If we must, we must."

He smiled down at her. "Excellent. Then shall we continue our tutoring?"

She sighed again, thwarted on all sides. "I suppose you will insist on that as well."

"Am I such a tyrant?" he teased, hoping to lighten her mood.

"Yes," she snapped, but as always it was impossible not to smile in response to his gamin grin. "No. As I said, if we must, we must. Have your toes quite recovered from yesterday?"

"You are as light as a feather and I never felt a single pain." He turned and limped convincingly toward the doorway. "Shall we?"

Laughing, she followed him into the hall.

Fiching obligingly fetched Miss Tindale, who was pressed into service at the pianoforte again. They practiced for some time, but although Eugennia acquitted herself far better than on the previous day, Kevin could tell her agile mind was elsewhere. Besides, the crowded room was getting on his nerves. When Miss Tindale stopped to shuffle the sheet music, Kevin drew Eugennia to his side.

"Do you truly have no ballroom, in all this huge town house?" he asked.

"Of course we do," Eugennia answered. "I saw no need to use it as I'm sure it's quite dusty. I've never had cause to go there."

"Well, you do now," Kevin declared. Miss Tindale eyed him, and he smiled innocently. She bent her gray head once more.

He lowered his head to speak in Jenny's ear. "Let's leave

your guardian dragon to her devices. Show me this ball-room."

He was doing it again, Jenny thought. He was using his charm to get her to do something on the edge of propriety. Well, she had certainly broken a few rules in the last day or so. She was within her rights to refuse him, but she didn't want to. She took his hand and tiptoed out of the room.

She led him upstairs to the back of the house to a set of double doors recessed in the paneled wall. Pushing one side open, she glanced in the shadowy room beyond and grimaced. "Just as I suspected. No one has been in here in ages."

Kevin peered over her head. The room was long and narrow, with arched windows running along one side and massive gilt-framed mirrors the other. By the light coming from the open door, he could see several dark credenzas under the mirrors, brass candelabra scattered along their dusty tops. The parquet floor was filmy with grit.

"Can we open the curtains?" he asked.

Jenny raised her skirts and walked across the floor, her steps leaving a trail in the dust, her passing echoing to the frescoed ceiling high above. She pulled back the first of the dark rose velvet drapes and dust danced in the sunlight, shimmering like fairy magic about her.

"How's that?" she asked, looking back at him. The sunlight turned her hair to gold, her skin to cream. It darkened her eyes and outlined her curves.

"Beautiful," he breathed.

Jenny blushed under his regard. He crossed the space to her side, gazing down at her.

"I thought we were going to dance," she tried when he had stood so for some time. Her heart was beating as if she had already danced a full card of lively country dances, and her breath came just as quickly.

"Ah, yes, dancing," Kevin replied, noting the way she bit her full lower lip. The temptation to kiss her was strong, but he fought it, at least for the moment. He raised his head to glance about the room, then smiled down at her. "Can you waltz, Miss Welch?"

She raised her eyebrows. "Waltz? I don't recall that one. Is it new?"

"Relatively so," he agreed. "I understand it is all the rage in Vienna right now. Would you like to try it?"

"Is it difficult?" she frowned.

"For my brilliant bluestocking, never. Let me show you." To her surprise, he took her hand with his right hand and slid his left about her waist.

"Are you sure this is how it is done?" she asked suspiciously.

Kevin grinned and tugged her closer to his body, as before, enjoying the feel of her. "Very sure. It is quite unlike any other dance you might have been taught. Now, watch my feet." He released her just enough so she could look down between them. "Like this."

He moved through the steps slowly and Jenny stumbled along with him. After a few movements, however, she tromped on his boot. Embarrassed, she shrugged out of his hold.

"I don't think I can do this," she shook her head.

"Nonsense," Kevin proclaimed, pulling her back into his embrace. "You'll do well if you just remember not to try so hard. For once in your life, don't think. Just react."

"Don't think?" Jenny laughed. "Better ask the sun not to shine than to ask a bluestocking not to think."

"Pretend it's a rainy day," Kevin countered. "Or better yet, close your eyes."

Jenny grimaced. "You aren't overly fond of your toes, are you?"

"Very well, then, look up, into my eyes."

I should have left well enough alone, she thought, but she took a deep breath and did as he suggested. Almost immediately, she was drawn into the lapis depths. She felt Kevin start to move and simply let her body follow. They glided down the room, swirling in and out of the dust-glittering sunlight and soft gray shadow. Her skirt belled against his Hessians. Her body swayed to his rhythm.

"Turn your head to the right," he murmured, and she turned to see a graceful couple dancing against the light. The gentleman was tall and imposing, his lady elegant and curvaceous. They spun back up the room, and she swore she heard her quartet playing in the background.

Kevin slowed his steps and she returned her gaze to his handsome face. He tightened his grip on her waist, never taking his eyes off hers. She swayed toward him as he lowered his head. With a groan, Kevin pulled her close and kissed her thoroughly, caressing her tender mouth with his own, feeling the curve of her against his chest and thigh. As before, she wanted the kiss to go on forever, pulling him closer, impossibly closer.

After a moment, he raised his head and gazed down at her. "Marry me, Jenny. I think I'll go mad if you don't."

She wanted to say yes. Oh, how she wanted to say yes! When he held her like this, and gazed down at into her eyes as he was doing, all her doubts vanished like puddles that could not withstand the heat of the sun. Saying yes in his arms was all too easy. Like dancing while looking up into his eyes, the response was reacting, not thinking. And a bluestocking could only hold back the thoughts for a very short time.

So, what would her answer be if she used her mind

rather than her heart? The facts on Kevin Whattling were still too few to tell whether the charming manner was real or counterfeit. The way he had declared his supposed love in the park had certainly been a different side of the man. Many people reacted so intensely in difficult situations, she knew, but how could she be sure that she had not just seen his true character?

Whichever way she analyzed it, she returned to the matter of her fortune. If he was sincere that he would marry her had he no need for it, then she would find it easier to believe his other claims. The only way to know was to see how he responded when he won the purse she had put up.

"Ask me after the fight," she murmured.

Kevin could see the struggle in her eyes. He almost cried out when he realized he hadn't won yet. Something still kept her from him. He wasn't sure what else he could do. He only knew he had to keep trying. He let go of her and bowed.

"As you wish, Madam. I think perhaps you've had enough lessons for one day. I will see you tomorrow night, when it will be my pleasure to escort you to Almack's."

Twenty

As if Kevin's fight and her debut at Almack's weren't enough to concern her, Jenny received the long-awaited report from Mr. Carstairs, her solicitor, that next morning. She almost didn't go down when Mavis came up to announce him.

"It doesn't matter what he says," she protested to Martha. "It won't change my feelings for Kevin Whattling one jot."

"It may not change your feelings," Martha replied, propelling her toward the door, "but at least you will go into your marriage with your eyes wide open. That's more than most women can say."

Jenny shook her head, but she continued toward the stairs with Martha at her heels. If nothing else, it was amusing to hear Martha assume that Jenny would marry Kevin. She wished she could be so sure of the outcome.

Mr. Carstairs was awaiting them in the library. He rose when they entered and bent over both their hands in turn, long nose twitching. He was a craggy man with a spare frame and sharp eyes. She had never noticed before that he habitually wore knee breeches, even in the early morning. Hanging about with a fashionable gentleman like Kevin Whattling had at least taught her that most gentlemen were wearing trousers these days. Carstairs nodded at her as she took her seat behind her father's desk.

"I have the report you requested on Mr. Whattling," he began. "I thought you would want to hear the results."

"Certainly," she acknowledged, ignoring Martha's smirk. "Please continue."

"Very well, Madam." He reached into his leather satchel on the floor beside his chair and selected a piece of paper. "Mr. Whattling is of a well-respected family from York-shire," he noted, blue eyes scanning the page. "His father had a small unentailed estate, which went to his wife, Mr. Whattling's mother, on his death. I cannot find a record of her death. I suspect she may have remarried so the name has changed. However, I did find a record of the sale of the estate approximately eighteen years ago. Mr. Whattling drew a small living from those proceeds until recently, when he emptied the account. He also recently auctioned off all his belongings, including a sizable stable. He currently has no visible assets and personal debts amounting to over two thousand pounds. He recently paid off debts of a considerably higher amount. Most likely this is why he sold the other items." He peered down the sheet, squinting at the handwriting. "No, that isn't quite correct. The debts he paid belonged to a Mr. Greene, Mr. Robert Greene."

Eugennia listened quietly. Nothing he had said surprised her, nothing contradicted anything Kevin had said. There was only one piece of the puzzle missing. "And did you find out anything about this Mr. Greene?"

Carstairs squinted at the paper more closely. He glanced up at her and smiled. "And did I tell you you are looking particularly lovely today, my dear? That shade of violet has always been quite becoming on you."

Miss Tindale smiled approvingly.

Eugennia scowled. "You only try that flummery on me when you do not want to tell me bad news. Pray answer the question."

Carstairs sighed. He reached back in the satchel and drew out a newspaper clipping. "Here, read it for yourself."

Eugennia took the piece of newsprint with some trepidation. *Boxer killed in illegal match,* the headline read. *Magistrates claim no fault.* She quickly scanned down the story, feeling Martha and Carstairs's eyes on her as she did so. Robert Greene had attempted to fight a man much larger and more experienced than he was and he had been killed by a blow to the head. The magistrates had determined that the gentleman who had arranged the match was not to blame. It was a great tragedy and perhaps the boxing world should be reformed, said *The Times.*

"What the paper does not say," Carstairs added as she handed the clipping to a rapt Martha, "is the relationship between Mr. Greene and Mr. Whattling. I take it he hasn't discussed the matter with you?"

Jenny shook her head. "No, and frankly, although I had heard something about Mr. Greene, it felt like prying to ask."

Carstairs raised an eyebrow. "Then you may not like the fact that I did pry. As you know, I'm not overly fond of mysteries, especially where my clients are concerned."

"If she doesn't want to know," Miss Tindale put in, glancing up from the clipping, "I do."

"Go on," Eugennia nodded in acceptance, although she felt her stomach doing unacceptable acrobatics again.

"Very well. I thought at first that Mr. Whattling was the gentleman who arranged the fight that cost young Greene his life. Why else would he take on the gentleman's debts? However, one of the investigators I hire for these issues learned that Mr. Greene was apparently Mr. Whattling's younger half brother. Unfortunately, as I lost track of Mrs. Whattling, I have not had time to find the evidence to prove her remarriage or the relationship between the two men."

"I am convinced your guess is correct," Eugennia replied firmly. She could feel sadness building inside her for the loss of a brother, and in such a manner. "You must be correct. That would explain too many remarks Mr. Whattling has made. How very sad for him."

"Little wonder he didn't want you watching boxing," Martha sniffed. Although it was her usual noise to indicate displeasure, Jenny noted that there were tears in her eyes as she handed the clipping back to Mr. Carstairs.

Carstairs acknowledged their agreement with a pert nod. "That he chose to honor his brother's debts does him credit. However, I am not impressed with his ability to handle the situation. I would say unlike many men, he appears to be more likely to lead with his heart."

"My exact opposite," Eugennia replied thoughtfully. She had realized it sooner, but Carstairs had summarized it nicely. Perhaps that was why she and Kevin were well matched. Everyone needed both a heart and a head to survive.

"This is not an issue to brush aside," Carstairs put in firmly. "Every bit of information I have gathered about the man indicates that he is too precipitous. However pleasant this fellow may be, I must caution you, Miss Welch, that this gentleman is not a good business risk. I would not want to see you invest any money in him."

Miss Tindale snorted. Jenny scowled at her.

Carstairs glanced between the two of them. "I am too late? Have you already agreed to fund this gentleman on some adventure?"

Jenny shook her head as Miss Tindale handed him back the clipping. "No, Mr. Carstairs. But I thank you for your trouble."

Carstairs nodded, tucking his papers back in his satchel. Miss Tindale watched him with growing concern.

"Wait," she ordered when he looked as if he were going to take his leave. She glanced at Jenny and sat a little straighter. "Eugennia, you might as well know all. Mr. Carstairs, I have read that when a lady marries, all her monies and goods become the property of her husband. Is that true?"

Jenny started. She had never thought about the fact that marrying Kevin might give him control of her fortune. "Yes, please, Mr. Carstairs, tell me."

He eyed the two of them. "Am I to take it that you are considering marrying this Whattling fellow?"

Eugennia found it impossible to meet his direct gaze. "I may marry someone, eventually."

Martha rolled her eyes.

"Of course you may," Carstairs agreed readily. "Your father and I discussed just such a possibility. While I believe we could protect some of your personal belongings, the sapphires for example and your other jewels, and a few of the books your father left you, I'm sorry to say that Miss Tindale is correct. When you marry, all control of your fortune becomes your husband's."

Jenny stared at the desktop, stunned. She should have thought to check sooner, but she had never seriously considered marriage before. And somehow, the law had never been a topic she had wanted to study.

"All the more reason for you to be very sure of the gentleman you marry," Carstairs continued, not unkindly. "Your entire life, everything you hold dear, you would be placing in his trust. That is a very serious matter, my dear."

"Very serious indeed," Martha echoed.

Jenny nodded. "Yes, I understand." She roused herself with difficulty. "Thank you again, Mr. Carstairs. I will think about everything you have said. And if I decide to marry, I hope I may call on your services to draw up the papers to protect my personal belongings, as you suggested."

"Of course, my dear," Carstairs assured her. "Whatever you desire."

But of course it wasn't what she desired, she thought as Fiching saw him out. Much as she would have liked to be annoyed at Martha for bringing up the subject, she agreed that it was best that she knew the truth. When she married, everything she owned, everything she held dear, became the property of her husband. She had feared, and hoped, loving Kevin Whattling might change her life. This was not the kind of change she had had in mind.

And she still wasn't satisfied that she knew the truth about Robert Greene. Based on Gentleman Jackson's stories, she would have said it was George Safton who had arranged the fateful match that had cost Robbie Greene his life. Was that the reason for the enmity between Safton and Kevin? She knew the only way to get an answer was to ask Kevin directly, but she couldn't seem to find the courage to face him, given the recent news and their upcoming appointment with the doyens of Almack's.

By the time Kevin arrived to escort her that evening, Eugennia felt as if she would surely expire from a severe strain to her nerves. She had never found anything that would overtax her active mind to the point of swooning, but she was very much afraid that before the night was out she would collapse. There were simply too many things competing for her attention. First she had to face the famed patronesses of Almack's and prove to herself and them that she knew how to behave in London society.

While Kevin's tutoring had made her feel a bit more confident, she still expected to be baited or even scorned on sight.

Worse, she much feared that news of her agreement to sponsor the upcoming fight might somehow have reached society's ears. The ladies of Almack's would have been only too pleased to pass along the on-dit. Society would be even more scandalized than usual at her unorthodox behavior, and she wasn't certain how Kevin would react. Although she had dispatched Stevens with a note requesting Gentleman Jackson to keep her involvement a secret, she could not be sure how many others already knew or which one of them might think to pass along the information to the wrong person.

Then of course there was the issue with Mr. Greene. And the issue of her fortune going to her husband. And the fact that Kevin might be hurt in the upcoming fight. Even she could not be expected to keep so many thoughts in her mind! Like a juggler with too many pins, she felt fumble-finger and lame. It did not bode well for the evening.

To make matters worse, the gown she had purchased for the event was entirely unsuitable to her. Martha gushed over the delicate gold-frosted lace on the bodice and sleeves, but all Jenny could see was how much of her chest and shoulders it left bare. Martha exclaimed over the graceful full skirt of pale cream silk that would sway when Jenny danced (if she got the courage to dance) but Jenny felt self-conscious at the way it seemed to call attention to her curves. With matching cream long gloves and pearls at her throat and ears, she felt barely presentable. The glint of appreciation in Kevin's dark eyes as she descended the stair to his side, however, told her Martha had been right.

"The bluestocking in gold," he smiled approvingly. "They will never let you return."

She felt her color draining and plucked at her skirt, dismayed that she had misunderstood the look in his eyes. "Is it as bad as all that?"

Kevin caught her hand, bending to meet her downcast gaze. "Of course not! You mistake me. You look so splendid that they will not be able to stand your glittering presence more than once."

"You are an impossible flatterer, Mr. Whattling," Jenny sighed with a shake of her head, but she felt her confidence increase with his praise. "One never knows when to believe you."

He raised her hand to his lips. "Always believe me, Jenny. I would never lie to you." She could feel the pressure of his kiss and the warmth of his breath through her glove. She snatched her arm back before goose flesh could form. Kevin raised an eyebrow.

"We wouldn't want to be late," she offered in explanation, motioning Fiching forward with her navy cloak. "Will someone fetch Miss Tindale?"

Kevin refused to be rebuffed. If his presence still disconcerted her, then perhaps he was closer than he had thought to winning her. He took the cloak from a surprised Fiching and draped it about Jenny's bare shoulders, letting his glove glaze her skin. She shivered and tugged the cloak closer about her.

"So sorry to be late," Miss Tindale cried, hurrying down the stairs. Fiching helped her into the black velvet cloak that lay waiting, the folds swallowing up the lighter gray of her plain satin dress.

"You did remember the vouchers, my dear?" she asked Jenny.

"Right here in my reticule," Jenny assured her. How

easy it would have been to misplace them, she thought as Kevin offered her and Martha his arms. She'd have much rather faced Countess Lieven's displeasure than Kevin Whattling's charm just then.

Twenty-one

It was interesting, Eugennia thought that night when she was lying in her bed, that the things which one feared most were generally not so terrible when faced directly. Almack's had proven to be one of those things. Instead of the censure she had expected to find, she had actually enjoyed herself. She had acquitted herself well the three dances she had danced. (She had noted that no one was waltzing, which supported her supposition that Kevin had made the dance up himself.) And for the most part, the conversations had been pleasant, if as innocuous as most society conversations generally were.

"Is this all there is to it?" Jenny had whispered to Kevin at one point in the evening, after she had chatted with Countess Lieven and Lady Jersey for several minutes between sets.

His lapis eyes twinkled. "Disappointed?" he whispered back. "Now do you see why I say you need not worry about making an impression on these people? My dear Jenny, you are the jewel to their paste imitations."

She had felt herself coloring and had been glad when another couple wandered up to discuss politics.

The one upsetting event of the evening had had nothing to do with her performance. Even as they had arrived at Almack's, the rooms had been buzzing with the news that

Napoleon had escaped Elba and was even now marching toward the French capital. The diplomats had been recalled from Vienna, and rumor had it that Wellington would soon be once more leading the English army into battle. Jenny was ashamed to admit that she was still more concerned for Kevin's safety in the upcoming fight than what might happen on some distant shore. In the last few months, her priorities had certainly changed.

Lying on Nigel's old army bedroll in his near-empty apartment, Kevin was also thinking about the evening. The news from abroad was disturbing. He was even more glad he hadn't taken Lord Hastings's offer to become a spy in France. And as for Jenny's performance that evening, she had been every bit the lady he knew she was capable of being. He could see it in the eyes of every peer and peeress they had met. Some had been delighted, others disappointed that she wasn't more of an oddity. He had wanted to hoist her up on his shoulders and proclaim her champion of the ring. As that was singularly inappropriate (and would have earned her the scorn she had originally feared), he decided to settle on flowers the next day. He had never been overly fond of the onyx stick pin his mother had given him. Selling it would give him enough money for the flowers and dinner for the next couple of nights.

He had to win her. With each advancing day it became more clear to him that he needed her. She made him think before acting. He had never considered it before, but in her presence it had become evident that he was too precipitous. He reacted rather than thinking through the situation. Had he been married to Eugennia when Robbie had first come to him with his gambling debts, he had little doubt things would have ended differently. It was little wonder he had fallen in love with her. Now all he had to do was convince her that she was in love with him.

Still in a celebratory mood, Kevin arrived at Eugennia's in the early afternoon, but to his surprise he found none other than Gentleman Jackson himself on the sitting room sofa, calmly sipping lemonade with Miss Tindale at his side and Eugennia across from him. Jenny at least had the good sense to look embarrassed, as he handed her the flowers, that he would find her in such company. Miss Tindale offered him a rather saucy smile, as if she enjoyed being the one to shock for once.

Kevin recovered himself and bowed over first Eugennia's and then Miss Tindale's hand. Eugennia tried not to look flustered by the frown on his face. It was her home, after all, and he wasn't her husband yet. He had nothing to say about whom she invited to visit.

"Mr. Jackson was explaining to us the circumstances of your upcoming fight with Mr. Safton," Miss Tindale told Kevin as he was seated. Eugennia tried not to notice that this only caused his frown to deepen. "I must say, I never knew it was all so complicated."

"She is referring to the umpires and the setting up of the ring," Eugennia explained. "We did not realize the bout had been moved out of London because of the expected crowd."

He raised his eyebrows. "Neither did I. Odd that Safton didn't think to let me know."

Gentleman Jackson shook his head. "Are you truly surprised? Then you are the only one, sir. I do not like to speak ill of any man, but for George Safton, I could make an exception. He was only too glad to have the bout moved from my rooms, out from under my direct supervision. I could hardly stop him. The wagering is simply too frenzied. The magistrates would have forced me to close."

"But surely they would have little interest in a amateur bout between two gentlemen," Kevin protested. "I can understand the wagering, sir, and if you say you think there will be a crowd, I will not gainsay you. However, this is hardly a championship fight. There isn't even a purse."

Eugennia started and looked at Jackson askance. Kevin felt as if he had been punched in the stomach as the realization hit. "Eugennia Welch, you didn't!"

She blanched, and even Miss Tindale quailed.

"There is a purse, Mr. Whattling," Jackson answered, glancing between the two of them. "And it doesn't matter who put it up."

"Of course it matters!" Kevin thundered, surging to his feet. "You know as well as I do that this fight could get ugly. I refuse to take money for it, hers or anyone else's."

Jenny wanted to sink into the sofa. His reaction was even worse than she had feared. Still, if putting up the purse would help Jackson catch Safton and protect Kevin, she could not back down now.

"If you win, you can refuse the purse, of course," Jackson replied calmly. "But I'd think about it if I were you. It's an impressive pot, lad, one of the largest I've seen. You could clear your debts and live well for years to come."

Kevin stared at him, mind whirling. He knew Jenny was worth a great deal, but even she would surely have had difficulty raising the kind of blunt Jackson was talking about. "Then it cannot be all Miss Welch's money," he protested.

To Eugennia's surprise, Jackson nodded. "That's correct. Several others have approached me as well, and I'm sure I'll get a few more before Friday. I can get you the exact amount if you like in a day or so. I just thought you should know."

Kevin nodded, dazed. Could this odious fight with

Safton really serve to clear all his debts? He hated to profit by it; it felt too much like blood money. But if he could truly settle all his debts and have something to build upon for the future, how could he in good conscience refuse? He could live a normal life again. He could hold his head up in public. He wouldn't have to offer his services to the Crown. And he wouldn't have to marry for money.

Eugennia watched the emotions pass across his handsome face and tried not to cry aloud. So, it was true. Despite all his protests to the contrary, he was willing to take any route to clear his debts. And now that he had another choice besides marrying, he would have no use for her. She had fooled herself all along into thinking he might actually care for her. There were times she believed he might even have fooled himself. Now they both knew it for the lie it was. She could hardly bear to look at him.

Kevin's eyes focused on Eugennia's face, and he realized she was miserable. He blinked, surprised, wondering what he had missed in his moment of introspection. He couldn't very well ask her in front of Gentleman Jackson and Miss Tindale. As it was, he had to suppress an urge to take her onto his lap and smooth the hair from her face.

As if nothing had happened, Miss Tindale clapped her hands. "How very splendid! Now we shall have even more to look forward to hearing about after the match."

Eugennia shook herself out of her despair. "After the match, Martha? Surely we will be *at* the match."

She still looked ashen to Kevin and he didn't like upsetting her anymore, but he had to depress any notions she had regarding the fight.

"Surely you will not," he replied firmly. "We've had this conversation before, Miss Welch. A boxing match is no place for a lady. Even Gentleman Jackson here will agree with me on that score."

To his surprise, the Gentleman eyed Eugennia, whose jaw was set with determination. "We've also talked of this before, Miss Welch. You know the threat to your reputation. Why do you want to watch this fight?"

Eugennia opened her mouth to declare that nothing would prevent her from watching a villain like George Safton be put down by the man she loved, then snapped her mouth shut. Under the circumstances, she could hardly say it. It shook her to realize she still meant it. Even though she felt he would never love her, it didn't change a thing. Kevin was watching her closely, and so was Jackson for that matter. She squared her shoulders. "I believe I told you, Mr. Jackson, that boxing is currently my field of study. How else am I to progress if I never actually witness the sport?"

He quirked a smile. "How else indeed, Madam. I encourage my lads to watch fights as they're learning."

"You cannot encourage her!" Kevin protested. "Much as you love the sport, Gentleman, I have never seen you bring a lady to a match. You cannot sit by and expect me to allow Miss Welch to attend."

Jackson grinned up at him. "I don't see that you have all that much to do with it, my lad. It is entirely up to Miss Welch."

Eugennia put her head up and glared at him, daring him to say otherwise. Kevin glared back.

"But you should know, Miss Welch," Jackson continued, "that Whattling is correct about one thing: the crowd will be no place for a lady."

"But surely there will be other women there," Eugennia protested. "You told me there were even other women who boxed."

"Women," Kevin snorted, "but hardly ladies. You'll be

accosted by half of the riffraff of London. A real lady would have nothing to do with the boxing."

She felt herself tremble in mortification. "And am I to assume that you no longer consider me a lady because of my study of the sport?"

"Of course not," he snapped, running a hand back through his hair in frustration. "How can I make you understand? You've heard yourself that the crowd is expected to be large. You'd be surrounded by pickpockets, drunks, and ladies of ill repute. I can hardly protect you while I'm fighting, and I don't like the thought of you alone in such a crowd. Egads, woman, I wouldn't even be able to concentrate on the fight if I thought you were in danger!"

She should have been touched, but at the moment his concern sounded more like self-preservation than anything else. Still, she supposed he did need to concentrate. She did not want to do anything that might give George Safton the upper hand.

"I'm sure Mr. Whattling can be counted on to give us a good accounting of the match," Miss Tindale offered.

"Of course. And I promise to come straight here after the match and tell you everything."

Eugennia knew she could not win the argument, not with Martha looking at her so pleadingly, Gentleman Jackson frowning at her, and Kevin glowering. She offered him the most insipid smile she could manage. "I can only say, Mr. Whattling, that I will look forward to your account."

Martha relaxed, but the answer didn't satisfy Kevin. Still, he could hardly press the issue with the Gentleman in the room. "It may not satisfy your intellectual curiosity, my dear," he offered in condolence, "but you will be far safer."

Jackson nodded, rising. "That settles it then. Miss Welch, I must be off. Thank you again for the hospitality. Miss

Tindale, your servant. Mr. Whattling, I'll look forward to seeing you at practice later."

Eugennia and Martha smiled politely and Kevin nodded in return as Fiching showed him out, the butler taking the flowers from Kevin with him. Kevin realized he should go as well, but he had too many issues to clear up to do so with an easy mind. And he could hardly raise them with Miss Tindale sitting there regarding him with the hair on her mole standing at attention again.

"Miss Tindale," he started, sitting back down on the chair, "I wonder how your notes have been coming regarding Miss Jenny's study of boxing."

"Miss Welch's study is going well," she sniffed. The correction of Jenny's name was not lost on him. If he had risen in Martha's regard over the last few weeks, he had obviously lost any ground he had gained. "And I am not going to leave this room to get my notes, a book on the subject, or *The London Times,* so you might as well not ask."

Kevin raised an eyebrow in innocent surprise at her response. Jenny shook herself. She couldn't be alone with Kevin, not now, perhaps not ever again.

"Of course not, Martha," she murmured. "No one would ask that of you."

As she *had* asked that of her companion any number of times, Kevin knew he was in deeper trouble than he had thought. "Very well, then, I suppose I'll simply have to state my case before both of you. Miss Welch, I would ask you to withdraw your support of this fight."

She blinked, then shook her head. Why did part of her persist in expecting him to make some kind of declaration now that he knew his debts would be paid without her? Of course he had nothing personal to say to her that would require Martha to leave. The time of stolen kisses and waltzes in shadow and sunlight was over. She had to make herself realize it.

Kevin took her silence as refusal. "Please, Jenny," he tried, reaching across the space to take her hands. She pulled them back out of reach, and Miss Tindale scowled at him so he thought she might stab him with her ever-present embroidery needle. He gave up and rose.

"Very well, have it your own way. I refuse to take your money. If I should win this fight, I will find out from Gentleman Jackson how much of the purse is yours and see that you get every penny back. I have a chance to clear my debts honorably, and I'm not going to loose it."

And of course, the dishonorable thing would have been to marry her for her money. She couldn't face him another second. "Very well, Mr. Whattling. Thank you for dropping by. Good luck on your fight with Mr. Safton. I somehow doubt you will need it."

She had never been so clear about dismissing him. He supposed she still smarted from his refusal to let her watch the fight. He rose and bowed. "Thank you, Madam. And I reiterate, I will stop by after the fight and let you know how it went." He wanted nothing so much as to declare himself again, but Miss Tindale's presence was hardly conducive. He settled on a subtle hint, hoping Jenny would realize what he meant. "And I believe we will have something to discuss then as well, something you requested me to ask you after the match."

Jenny stared at him, afraid to hope. But there had been only one thing she had asked him to ask her after the match. "As you wish, Mr. Whattling," she managed.

It wasn't the best of answers, but he'd have to settle for it. He bowed again and allowed Fiching to show him out.

"You cannot say that man isn't interesting," Martha

noted, finishing a knot and snipping off the thread with silver scissors.

"No, you can't," Jenny allowed, mind and emotions in turmoil. It appeared she might have a chance after all, but her bruised heart was too tender to allow her much hope. Still, some hope was better than none at all. As soon as her butler returned to the sitting room, she turned to him thoughtfully.

"So, Fiching, how would one go about getting seats for Mr. Whattling's boxing match?"

Martha gasped. "Eugennia, no! Mr. Whattling told you it was no place for a lady. Will you not listen for once?"

"Rubbish," Eugennia sniffed with a toss of her head. "I do not believe all that folderol about pickpockets and cutpurses. Lord Byron boxes, for pity's sake!"

"A great number of lords box, Miss Jenny," Fiching put in with a thoughtful frown. "That doesn't make them gentlemen. We'd have to be mighty circumspect."

"Fiching!" Martha cried. "How can you encourage her!"

"Simply because nothing either of you will say will discourage me," Eugennia informed them. "This whole fight started because of an insult to me. I have also put up considerable money for the event." *Not to mention my own heart,* she amended to herself. "If you think I will miss it, you don't have the sense I credited you with."

Twenty-two

With continued protests from Martha and grudging assistance from Fiching, Eugennia managed to find a way after all. A good two hours before the match was slated to begin the next day, she was dressed in Stevens's footman's uniform and perched beside Fiching in the driver's box of her closed carriage, overlooking what had been an empty field just north of London.

"Well, he certainly was right about the crowd," she murmured to Fiching as she scanned the milling people between her and the tramped square of dirt where the fight would take place. It was roughly an eight-foot square, about which someone had hung rough rope suspended on stakes pounded into the turf. The makeshift barricade did not stop the people from crowding close. From her perch above them, she could see elegant gentlemen in top hats and greatcoats, shabbily dressed fellows in tweeds and breeches, and several climbing boys in their dirt and grime alongside their masters. Bottles passed among the knots of men, and already she could see red noses and hear laughter that was overly loud. Someone on her right was selling brandy balls, the singsong call rising and falling over the conversations. To her left came the aroma of hot roasted chestnuts.

"He was right about the ladies as well," Fiching murmured beside her, waving toward the field. "Not a proper chit in sight."

"Nonsense," Eugennia started to protest. She could see any number of women threading their way through the crowd. Their presence made her wonder why she had bothered to masquerade as a man. Stevens's top hat barely fit over her tucked-up hair, but his uniform was loose enough to hide her curves. Unfortunately, it was heavy and hot in the March sunshine. She would almost have preferred to dress as lightly as the ladies below. Then she looked again.

The ladies were not ladies after all. This one's bodice had an alarmingly low décolletage, that one's dress was obviously several sizes too small, and at least two of them had damped their petticoats so that their thin muslin dresses clung to their curves. The woman nearest the square was obviously quite cold, her nipples standing out against the fabric of her gown. Eugennia averted her gaze in a blush.

"Perhaps you're right," Fiching allowed. "There may be a lady or two in one of the other carriages."

Thankful for something else to look at, Eugennia glanced around. Hers was one of a number of vehicles circling the area, from high-perch phaetons to closed landaus. She thought she saw a crest on one of them.

"Marquess of Hastings," Fiching nodded when she pointed it out. "Wouldn't be surprised to find more than one gentleman from the War Office inside."

"Even with this tale of Napoleon's escape?" Jenny marveled. "One would think they had better things to do."

Fiching shrugged. "We beat him once, we'll do so again. Besides, Lord Hastings's son Lord Petersborough and his crowd are big fight supporters. I don't suppose they'd miss this even if old Boney was marching on London."

Jenny found she felt much the same way. The two hours passed more quickly than she had thought possible. Just as she was starting to get restless, there was a stir among the crowd and she saw a rider and the familiar white curricle arriving on the London road. She recognized the matched whites immediately.

"Sir Nigel Dillingham," Fiching told her. "And the round-faced chap beside him is Giles Sloane."

"We've met," Eugennia replied, recognizing the thatch of red hair as well. The rider on the bay was the one who held her interest. Kevin waved as he approached, and the crowd cheered. Eugennia felt a surge of pride that made her straighten in her seat. The action unfortunately threatened to topple the hat from off her head. She quickly ducked back down behind Fiching in case Kevin should notice her.

He looked magnificent as always in a navy coat of superfine and fawn trousers. He doffed his top hat at the cheer, sunlight glinting off his golden hair. She couldn't seem to take her eyes off him as he moved through the people to the square.

"Opera glasses, Miss Jenny?" Fiching offered, and she snatched them from his gloved hand, focusing them on Kevin. He was smiling and joking with someone at the side of the square. He paused to doff his hat again, and she saw that the woman in the thin muslin dress had now arranged her still-freezing body for his review. Jenny dropped the glasses into her lap.

Another carriage arrived, an equally fine equipage with brown enameled sides. It was pulled by a pair of prancing blacks. George Safton, in black cloak and trousers, stood for the crowd's approval. She did not think it was her imagination that made the cheer seem much less enthusiastic.

Fiching picked up the glasses from her lap and applied them himself. "So, that's The Snake. Looks like he's ready for this."

Even without the glasses, Eugennia could see the confidence as Safton strode to the square, shrugging off hands that reached out to him in good will. He ducked under the ropes, coming up with a swirl of his black cloak. He took it off with a flourish. Eugennia sucked in a breath.

Fiching looked at her askance. "Something wrong, Miss Jenny?"

"The books didn't say they'd be bare-chested," she managed. She was almost afraid to look, but when she did, she saw that Kevin was peeling off his coat and shirt as well.

"Give me those," Eugennia snapped, grabbing the glasses from a startled Fiching. Training them on the square, she saw the ripple of muscle as Kevin pulled off his white lawn shirt, baring himself to the waist. His powerful shoulders and hardened arms seemed to glow in the sunlight. The flat plane of his stomach disappeared into the waistband of his form-fitting trousers. One of the "ladies" in the crowd whistled. Kevin grinned at her. Eugennia hastily returned the glasses to Fiching, face flaming.

Two men appeared from the crowd and joined Safton on his side of the square. Giles and Nigel joined Kevin on his.

"The seconds," Fiching explained, although she had read about it in her studies. "They'll serve as time-keepers and they'll help their chaps during breaks. Those two"— he pointed to two burly gentlemen who had approached the square, the crowds giving way before them—"are the umpires. They're ex-fighters brought in to make sure everything is fought fairly."

Jenny nodded, relaxing a little. Surely Safton would have little opportunity to harm Kevin with two such gentlemen in attendance. As she watched, one of the umpires strode to the center of the square and drew a line in the dirt with his toe. He nodded to Safton and Kevin, who joined him in the center. He asked them a question. Safton shrugged. Kevin shook his head.

"He wants them to shake hands," Fiching put in helpfully. "Mr. Whattling apparently refused."

"Serves Mr. Safton right," Jenny agreed.

Below, there was a few moments' discussion; then the umpire stepped back.

"Gentlemen," he called for the crowd's benefit, the deep voice echoing across the hushed field. "I give you a bare-knuckle bout between Mr. Kevin Whattling and Mr. George Safton." Another cheer went up, nearly drowning his last words. "Fighters, toe the mark."

Safton stood with arms raised in fists before him, and Kevin took up a similar stance across the line in the dirt. She thought Safton said something and saw Kevin stiffen. Then he laughed, resuming his pose. The umpire nodded, and they started circling.

The crowd grew still again, but only for a moment. Then voices began calling, exhorting Kevin and Safton to strike. They continued circling, watching each other, and Eugennia felt as if she couldn't breathe. Then George swung, and she gasped as Kevin blocked it.

They returned to circling, and the calls intensified. George jabbed, right, then left. Kevin blocked both easily. George dropped his guard and swung for the stomach. Kevin danced back out of reach.

The calls grew more numerous, and Eugennia noticed that those rooting for George had increased.

"Why doesn't he swing?" Fiching muttered, glasses glued to the view.

"He's sizing him up," Eugennia replied wisely. "He wants to exploit Mr. Safton's weakness."

"As if he had one," Fiching scoffed; then he lowered the glasses to offer Eugennia a contrite smile. "Sorry, Miss Jenny. No disrespect meant for Mr. Whattling."

"Do not doubt him, Fiching. Everything I have read, everything Mr. Jackson explained to me, tells me that he is doing everything right. He will triumph. It is only a matter of time."

Even as she finished her sentence, Kevin's arms flashed through Safton's guard, first right, then left, in quick succession. Safton staggered and went down on one knee. A cry went up, and the seconds hurried into the square. Two drew Safton away to the left. Nigel and Giles hurried to pull Kevin away to the right.

She did not have time to relax. The break lasted only half a minute before Safton and Kevin were once again in the center, squared off against each other. The dancing continued, but Safton was being more careful this time. She gasped as his fist connected with Kevin's nose and Kevin fell.

The seconds separated them again. Kevin perched on Giles's knee while Nigel squeezed an orange into his mouth. Safton pushed the fruit he was offered away.

"Arrogant toad," Eugennia muttered. Fiching grunted in agreement.

A half minute later they returned to the square. Thus it continued round after round. Sometimes Kevin managed to knock Safton off his feet. More often it was Safton who made the hit. Eugennia took the opera glasses from Fiching during the eighteenth round. As she had feared, Kevin's lip was bleeding, his left eye was beginning to swell, and sweat glistened on his chest. There was an ugly bruise forming on the underside of his left ribs. She bit her lip and lowered the glasses, almost afraid to watch any longer.

Down on the square, Kevin wasn't sure how much longer he could last. "No more," Kevin gasped, pushing away the orange Nigel offered him. "And no more of this either. I've got to finish him."

"You've got the right of it," Nigel agreed, waving a towel back and forth in front of him to help cool him. "Safton has the staying power of a percheron. You've got to end this, and quickly."

Kevin nodded, reaching for the water bottle. He guzzled down the tepid liquid and let it splash his face. It stung against his bruised eye and cut lip. Squinting with his right eye, he saw Giles watching him, round face puckered with concern.

"Buck up, my lad," he joked. "Haven't you told me how I can get myself out of any scrape?"

Giles managed a weak smile. "Yes, I have been known to say that. He just seems so intent on beating you, Kev. And beating you up in the process."

Kevin glanced across the square where Safton was refusing to sit on his kneeman. He strutted about his side of the square instead, glowering over at Kevin and his friends. The look had all the force of a malevolent creature stalking its prey. Kevin stood to return to the center.

"Had enough?" Safton sneered when they had taken up their places. "Will you give it up, or do I have to put you down like your brother?"

The bile rose in Kevin's throat, but he raised his fists and began to circle, forcing himself to concentrate. He would not let Safton bait him. Robbie's death in the boxing square had been a tragic accident, just as everyone kept telling him. He had never been able to prove any wrongdoing on Safton's part, much as he had wanted to. Losing his temper now would only put him farther into Safton's power.

George watched Kevin circling and seethed with frustration. Nothing he had done had so much as rattled the man. He was sure repeated mentions of his brother would madden Kevin beyond reason, yet here he was, just as cool as ever. There had to be something he could do to get him to lower his guard. Beyond the square, one of the doxies whistled at him. He smiled.

"When we're done here, Whattling," he called across the square, "I hope you'll give my regards to Miss Welch. Then again, perhaps you won't be in any condition to do so. I suppose I'll just have to comfort the lady myself."

Kevin took a deep breath, watching him and ignoring the words, though they settled like a hot coal in his stomach. The thought of this creature so much as touching his Jenny infuriated him. He squinted his eyes and hunkered lower.

It was working. George was sure he could see sweat standing out on Whattling's brow where none had been moments before. He didn't think it was the sun or the exertion this time. "Of course, she doesn't seem the type to enjoy comforting," he continued. "But then, perhaps she just hasn't met the right man yet."

He is too confident, Kevin thought, lowering his guard quickly to wipe the sweat from his stinging eyes. It was all an act. One lucky punch and the man would never go near Jenny again. All he had to do was keep his wits about him. He had to stop himself from merely reacting. He had to think.

Safton swung and Kevin danced back out of reach. But he was tired, and he stumbled. Safton leaped the distance, swinging hard. Once again his fist connected with Kevin's jaw, and Kevin stumbled back as the light dimmed.

"Time!" Giles screamed, and Nigel rushed in before Safton could close. Grinning, Safton allowed his seconds to lead him to his side of the square. Nigel carefully wiped the sweat from Kevin's brow with the towel, and Giles mumbled something about ending it.

"I'm all right," Kevin snapped, waving them away. He stood and stretched, making a show of how relaxed he was. George wanted him rattled. Well, when they returned to the square, perhaps rattled is what he would get. That ought to help open his guard a bit. Ignoring George's taunting grin from across the square, he allowed his gaze to sweep the crowd, taking in the wide eyes, the cheering mouths. He glanced at Lord Hastings's coach across the way, which he had spotted when they came in, and wondered how the old man was enjoying the show. It was quite a spectacle if the footman with the opera glasses was any indication.

He froze and stared, recognizing Fiching immediately. He had never seen any of Jenny's coaches, but it had to be hers. Then, as the footman lowered the glasses and ducked behind Fiching, the top hat tumbled off her dark blond hair.

"Damn the woman," he muttered. But Safton had taken up his place in the center, and Kevin had no choice but to join him.

"So, she couldn't resist, could she?" Safton jeered, jabbing at him. He stepped aside easily, trying without luck to get himself to calm. "I saw you looking at the coach. She's inside, isn't she? That's a bluestocking for you. They enjoy studying. I have quite a few tricks to teach her, I assure you. And I intend to enjoy every minute of it."

"Save your breath, Safton," Kevin snapped. He wanted

nothing more than to knock that satisfied smile off the man's face, but he had to watch for his moment. "Nothing you can say will change the fact that I'm going to beat you."

"Are you?" Safton lunged. Kevin tried to dodge, but Safton caught his arm, pinning him in place. As he turned to bring up his other arm in defense, Safton smashed him in the face. Pain shot through him. The day darkened again, and he felt his knees buckling. *Not now,* he swore. *Keep your wits about you. This is your opening. Think!*

Safton twisted the arm up over Kevin's head and leered down at him, his other hand poised to strike again.

"I've ruined you, Whattling. Are you ready to face that yet? I've ruined you, your brother, and now I'm going to ruin your Miss Welch. When I'm through with her, there won't be a man in England who will want her, even with her great fortune. And there's nothing you can do about it."

George had left himself wide open. Suddenly the day brightened and with a mad yell, Kevin swung his left arm upward. He put into it every ounce of strength he had left, every bit of frustration over Robbie's death, all the shame from his mounting debts, every fear for Eugennia's safety. He smashed his doubled fist into Safton's jaw and watched as the man dropped his arm and tumbled over backward to smack his head on the ground and lie still. There was one second of silence, and then the crowd erupted with cheers.

He couldn't seem to move off his knees as people swarmed around him. Nigel appeared on one side and Giles on the other, and somehow he was standing again. He thought he saw Gentleman Jackson beaming at the side of the square. Others crowded around, patting his back, shaking his hand. Someone shoved a tankard into his hand, and he swallowed the burning liquid down. Someone thrust a willing wench into his arms, and his bruised lip protested as she covered it with kisses. Her devotion nearly flattened him, but Nigel and Giles stepped in again, disengaging her and helping him through his well-wishers to the waiting carriage. It was all a bumble of noise and color, and he had passed out before he actually hit the squabs.

Twenty-three

It was Fiching who managed to get her into the carriage. When she saw Kevin collapse into the Dillingham coach, her first instinct was to dash to his side to help. Fiching barely convinced her that it was an ill-advised act.

"Look at the people swarming about, Miss," he urged. "Half of them are drunk as lords and the other half are wild to celebrate. You'll never reach him through that."

She craned her neck to see over the people who thronged about the white carriage. "But what if he's badly hurt? You saw that blackguard strike him again and again! He could be bleeding to death even as we speak."

"That I doubt, Miss," Fiching chided. "He promised you he'd come to see you as soon as he was able. Let Sir Nigel and Mr. Sloane set him to rights first. A Corinthian of Mr. Whattling's stripe won't much care to have his lady see him like this, I've no doubt."

She sighed, subsiding. Fiching was right. She could hardly reach him in this crowd, and even as she watched, Sir Nigel was starting to maneuver the carriage through the press back toward London. She would have to wait to see him.

If he came.

All the way home she kept telling herself that he would. He simply had to. She needed him to help her feel as well as think. And he needed her to think as well as feel. When the heart and the head were in accordance, nothing could gainsay them. Together, she and Kevin would both be better off. If only she could state her case as compellingly to his face!

She returned home, changed into her dove-colored silk gown, brushed out her hair, and instructed Martha to wait at least a half hour before coming downstairs to check on her. If Kevin arrived, she wanted time alone with him. If he didn't, she was sure she wouldn't be very good company. She was starting down the stairs to the sitting room when she heard the knocker sound on the front door. Fiching grinned at her as he hurried to open it.

"It appears the gentleman couldn't wait after all," he chuckled. He had barely pulled open the door when it was slammed into him. Fiching gasped and stumbled back, catching himself on the hall table. George Safton, mouth bloody, face bruised, strode into the entryway.

Eugennia stood frozen on the stair. Fiching struggled to his feet, but before he could call out to Stevens or any of the other servants, Safton smashed his fist into the man's mouth. Jenny cried out as Fiching crumbled to the floor.

"Good afternoon, Miss Welch," Safton declared, striding toward her. She scrambled back up the stairs away from him, mind whirling.

"Stevens! Jenkins!" she shouted, but Safton took the stairs two at a time and seized her about the waist. She struggled against him, kicking and slapping. Although he grunted at her exertions, his grip only tightened. Below stairs came the sound of pounding footsteps.

"It appears we are to be interrupted," Safton chided her. "And I so wanted to further our acquaintance." He raised her off her feet, pressing her against his chest, so that her eyes were level with his own. "Now, don't make me do anything I will regret later, my dear."

"Leave me alone!" she cried, wriggling in vain to escape his grip.

He started up the stairs, chuckling. "You are much more curvaceous than I had expected in a bluestocking. Keep that up and I'll have to more closely investigate this delightful flesh I'm feeling."

Jenny stopped, but she did not give up as Safton carried her down the upper hall. Voices were calling for her below, and it would be only a matter of minutes before her servants found her.

"Put me down this instant!" she insisted as he paused before an open door. "I warn you, Mr. Safton, you will not get away with this."

"Oh, but I will, Miss Welch," he sneered, maneuvering her through the door. He dropped his hold, and Eugennia scrambled away from him. He didn't pursue her, going instead to shut the door and wedge a chair under the handle. She glanced about the room, noting that they were in one of the little-used guest bedrooms. As it was over the music room, she had had a carpenter put padding in the floor as well as the walls to prevent the sound from traveling. Worse, from the pillows on the bed to the too heavy gilt-framed picture on the wall, there was nothing she might use as a weapon against him. Safton could not have chosen a better room if he had tried. She would not be able to use her wits. It was time to try Kevin's way. She squared her shoulders and put up her fists.

Safton turned back to her and took in her stance. He chuckled again. "Are you honestly trying to defend your honor that way? You saw me today, Miss Welch. For all your

Mr. Whattling managed to get a lucky punch, I am the superior fighter. You have no chance here."

"That, sir," she informed him, fists upraised, "is your opinion."

He took a step forward, eyes slits of malice. "Boo!"

She jumped, and he laughed. He took another step forward, and she circled away from him as she had seen Kevin do.

"This is ridiculous," he growled. "You may as well give up. Even if your servants find us, your reputation is in shreds. Do you honestly think Whattling will want you when I'm through with you?"

"Why are you doing this?" Jenny demanded, fighting the fear his words raised in her. "You don't want me. You cannot think you will somehow gain from this!"

"Oh, but I will gain, Miss Welch. Can you imagine how I felt coming to on the field to see the Bow Street Runners conversing with your friend Jackson and Kevin's two little toadies? I should have realized Sloane and Dillingham were up to something. It's obvious I'm finished. But, by God, Whattling will pay."

Behind him the door handle rattled.

"In here!" Jenny shouted. Safton lunged for her, and she danced out of reach. Cursing, he pursued her.

"Jenny!" Kevin's voice came muffled through the door. "Hang on!"

"Damn you, Whattling!" Safton shouted back. "You won't win this time!" He lunged at Jenny again, and she managed to dart under his reach. The door shuddered as shoulders slammed into it. Safton doubled his fists.

"I'm very sorry to end it this way, my dear," he murmured, drawing back an arm. "Goodbye, Miss Welch."

Jenny smashed her fist up under his guard, straight into

the underside of his chin. Pain shot through her hand. George blinked.

The door crashed open, splintering the chair. Kevin clambered over the wreckage into the room, Giles, Nigel, and her footmen close on his heels. George Safton swayed on his feet, eyes rolling back into his head. Before Kevin could reach him, he fell forward onto his face.

Jenny stepped back, shaking out her aching hand. "Interesting. Was that a jab or an upper cut?"

Kevin stared at her, a smile slowly spreading across his own bruised face. "Miss Welch, I take it all back. Boxing is definitely a sport for ladies."

Sometime later Jenny, Kevin, and Miss Tindale were all safely ensconced in the sitting room, cold compresses on Kevin's left eye and Jenny's hand. Fiching was being tended to by a doting Mavis, and Nigel and Giles were escorting Safton's unconscious body to Bow Street to meet a just punishment from the magistrates. Martha could only marvel at how it had all turned out.

"So Mr. Safton was responsible for pitting your brother against that monster," she concluded after both Kevin and Jenny had explained.

"And that's where this enmity with Safton began," Jenny added.

Kevin nodded. "Yes, although I hope you know I never thought he would go this far. I think my heart stopped beating the moment Giles and Nigel and I arrived and found Fiching on the floor and your name echoing above. It didn't start beating again until I knew you were safe. If anything had happened to you, Jenny . . ."

She blushed under his regard. "Nothing terrible happened. Everything came out all right in the end, just as you promised. Mr. Sloane and Sir Nigel were very clever to trap him that way."

"And very brave," Miss Tindale put in. "I'm sorry to admit I was taken in by the man. I don't know how they managed to get others to see through him."

"One of those cases that took both intellect and heart," Kevin agreed.

Jenny blushed, thinking of her own conclusions. "It has been made clear to me that both are needed for a good life."

"Or a good marriage," he murmured, watching her. "Which reminds me, we still have my suit to discuss. You must know I will not rest, Jenny, until you've agreed to marry me."

Jenny stared up at him, heart soaring. The sunlight from the windows behind them bathed him in a golden glow and even though he wore his usual navy coat and fawn trousers, she would have sworn he was dressed all in shining armor, every bit the handsome prince she had dreamed of. "You— you still want to marry me? Even though you won that purse?"

So that was what had been bothering her, Kevin realized. She thought that with money within his reach, he would have no further use for her. It was another of her notions that he had to put a stop to. Alone. He glared at Miss Tindale.

Martha jumped to her feet, obligingly taking the hint. "Oh, dear, I seem to have misplaced my puce thread. I'll be right back."

Eugennia rose as Martha hurriedly quit the room. In the back of her mind, she heard her companion close the door. Her eyes were only for Kevin, who reached for her and drew her to his side.

Kevin knew he ought to declare his undying devotion,

but he had ever preferred action to words. He pulled her onto his lap and into his embrace, leaving no doubt in her mind as to his feelings about her.

And then it was some time before the bluestocking on his knee could think clearly at all.

ABOUT THE AUTHOR

Regina Scott lives with her family in Kennewick, Washington, and is the author of two previous Zebra Regency romances: *The Unflappable Miss Fairchild* and *The Twelve Days of Christmas.* She is currently working on her fourth, *Catch of the Season,* which will be published in November, 1999. Regina loves to hear from readers and you may write to her c/o Zebra Books. Please include a self-addressed stamped envelope if you wish a response.